CHEAT
BOOK

belongs to:

_____

THE CHEAT BOOK

VOL·1

To Olivia

WRITTEN & ILLUSTRATED BY

RAMZEE

HODDER

HODDER CHILDREN'S BOOKS
First published in Great Britain in 2024 by Hodder & Stoughton

1 3 5 7 9 10 8 6 4 2

Text & illustrations copyright © RAMZEE, 2024

The moral right of the author has been asserted.

A CIP catalogue record for this book
is available from the British Library.

ISBN: 978 1 444 97338 9

Typeset in Mrs Eaves and Prater Block

Printed and bound in Great Britain by Clays Ltd, Elcograf S.p.A.

The paper and board used in this book
are made from wood from responsible sources.

MIX
Paper | Supporting
responsible forestry
FSC® C104740
FSC
www.fsc.org

Hodder Children's Books
An imprint of
Hachette Children's Group
Part of Hodder & Stoughton Limited
Carmelite House
50 Victoria Embankment
London EC4Y 0DZ

An Hachette UK Company
www.hachette.co.uk

www.hachettechildrens.co.uk

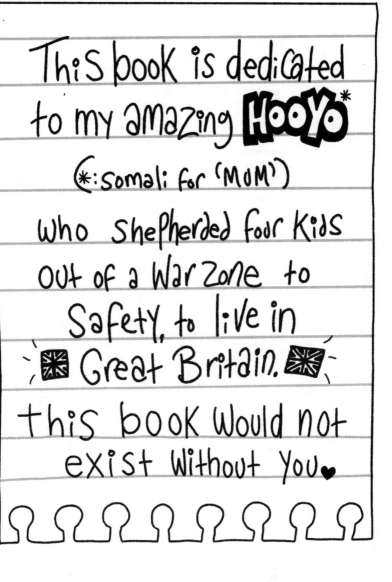

This book is dedicated to my amazing **HOOYO***

(*: Somali for 'MOM')

who shepherded four kids out of a warzone to safety, to live in Great Britain.

this book would not exist without you.♥

CHAPTER ONE

I don't know if you know this, but school is

→AWESOME!←

Not convinced?

Don't get me wrong, I'm not a 'first-hand-up, stationery-neatly-arranged-on-my-desk, reads-the-dictionary-for-fun' kid.

You know – a **DORK**.

For dorks, school is a theme park of knowledge where every class is a rollercoaster of learning. Where, when the day of fun challenges and exciting problem-solving is over, they're given party bags filled with treats called **'HOMEWORK'**.

ugh.

The smell of textbooks is enough to make me break out in a **STRESS RASH**.

So, no, I'm not a dork, but I'm not a **NORMIE** either.

Normies see school like an escape room that their parents have thrown them into. Where the only way out is to complete tasks before the final bell rings, or they'll get locked in detention for ever.

Sucks to be them.

Like I said, I'm neither a dork nor a normie, because I'm a **COOL KID** and, for me, school is a movie set and I am the **STAR**.

My typical school day goes like this:

I wake up and SLIDE out of bed

In the bathroom, I put on my 'morning headset'. A gadget that I invented that gets me ready for school.

Fortnite Highlights

Try and fail to dodge Mum's sloppy goodbye kisses (gross)

whilst grabbing the last falafel breakfast wrap (yum)

My chauffeur, Potsworth, picks me and Wing (my best friend) up in a Batmobile and rockets us to school in record time.

BRIXTON

I do my Cool Kid strut through the school gates, which makes all eyes swing over in my direction . . .

. . . and the chanting starts . . .

I can't take a single step down the school corridor without hearing:

Everyone wants a piece of me, even the caretaker – but I just want to get to class.

But not before I take a peek at the school noticeboard to see what's for dinner today:

MON

MENU

Two lumps of baked potato,
sausages (medium rare),
a glob of tapioca and a cup of milk.

KAMAL'S MENU:

Halal Chicken Wellington with mozzarella
and pesto. Roasted new potatoes with
green beans and gravy, baked vanilla
cheesecake topped with blueberry
compote and a glass of sparkling water.

The dinner ladies have really outdone
themselves. I'll have to get
them *another* **TEN-DAY CRUISE**
for Christmas.

The bell rings and now I'm in maths class with the kooky Mr Osterhaus, who always puts a maths 'joke' on the top corner of the whiteboard. Anyone in class who can guess the punchline wins a prize – usually a chocolate bar.

Mr Osterhaus

Some of Mr Osterhaus's previous 'hilarious' maths teasers:

Why did I divide sin by tan?

Which triangles are the coldest?

Why didn't a hyperbola feel sick?

And Zain Choudhry always gets them right. He shoots his hand up and says:

Just COS!

Ice-sosceles triangles!

It was Asymptote-matic!

This maths wizardry has earned Zain the nickname, **'ZAIN BRAIN'**.

But today, instead of a joke, Mr Osterhaus has scrawled a really strange bunch of symbols and letters on the corner of the whiteboard.

'Hey, sir. What's that?' I ask, pointing at it.

'Oh!' chuckles Mr Osterhaus, 'that's just something I wrote up as a joke. It's the Collatz conjecture. One of the hardest maths problems in the world.'

Zain frowns. No chocolate bar today.

I don't know what a conjecture is, let alone a Collatz one, but those strange symbols look weirdly familiar. Then it hits me where I know them from!

Last summer, at my mosque's youth group, we learned about famous Muslim scientists and scholars from history, and one of them was Al-Khwarizmi, who is called 'The Father of Algebra'. The imam (a Muslim scholar) made us write out one of his equations a **HUNDRED TIMES**.

I want you to know this as well as $E=MC^2$.

Back in maths class, I ask what the prize for solving the sum is, which makes Mr Osterhaus chuckle even harder. 'If you can solve this, nobody here has to go to another maths class ever again.'

No more maths? **EVER?**

'You're on, sir!'

The whole room falls silent as I walk over to the whiteboard. As soon as my pen touches the board, I am off. Like that of a painter at an easel, my pen flows and squeaks across the surface.

I don't even know what it means, but from the imam's endless drilling I know exactly where each squiggle and letter belongs.

My pen runs out and I pick up another one, and another. Until, finally, I am finished.

I turn to see a sceptical Mr Osterhaus, who then inspects what I've written against a textbook on his desk, vigorously scrutinising every **DOT** and **SQUIGGLE**, his eyes growing wider and wider, his jaw going lower and lower, until, astonished, he says, 'Well done, Kamal.'

The applause is **DEAFENING**!

Before I know it, I am swamped by ecstatic classmates who then all lift me up on their shoulders, chanting.

I love every second of it.

Who knew paying attention at mosque would pay off so well?

In the sea of clamouring faces I spot Keisha, the prettiest girl in class, and she is smiling right at **ME**!

I go all warm and loopy inside. But just as I am about to ask her to have lunch with me, something **WEIRD** starts happening. Orange hair starts **SPROUTING** out of her brown cheeks and her braids start to fall out of her head!

Her clothes start to **STRETCH** out and **MORPH** into a business suit.

Her brown skin turns pale and slightly pink.

I blink and suddenly my cheering classmates whose shoulders I was bouncing on, all vanish with a *poof* and I plummet to the floor, landing on my butt with an *ouch*!

I get up to find that not only was Keisha now Principal Jenkins but I was no longer in my maths classroom but standing centre stage in the school auditorium, with hundreds of eyes glaring at me.

Worst of all, I am no longer the coolest kid in school but, instead, an ordinary **NOBODY** kid who is about to read a poem in front of the entire school.

CHAPTER TWO

This is me

Observe the frown

Notice the bugged-out eyeballs of utter despair

The clammy forehead of sheer panic

Being shoved out in front of the entire school during assembly was enough to give me what the biology textbooks call **'STAGE FRIGHTUS'**.

I would've melted on the spot if the Head hadn't been up there with me.

'THE HEAD' is what us school kids call Principal Jenkins, on account of his massive bald head that changes colour depending on his mood. Which is usually angry.

He has a Temper Scale, which starts at Irritated Salmon and explodes at Raging Purple.

Right then, he was a Tense Lilac.

'Go on, son,' said the Head, gesturing to the microphone.

I shut my eyes and tried to escape back into my comforting daydream, but it was no use. My imagination had peaced out and left me stranded in the **REAL WORLD** with a mind that'd gone completely blank and a stomach that'd tied itself up in knots.

Why would anyone want to listen to my poem?

Everyone at Shackleton Academy would say that I am the **LEAST INTERESTING** kid that you could ever meet. Your basic, run-of-the-mill, bargain-basement kid. Ordinary. Bland.

In fact, people find me so average that I am hard to describe. Even my school reports all say: **'FAIR'**.

But that's exactly how I want it.

Because my average-ness is all an act.

SCHOOL REPORT
ENGLISH FAIR
MATHS FAIR
HISTORY FAIR
SCIENCE FAIR

You see, in a school full of thugs and sadistic teachers, sticking out is the fastest route to getting an atomic wedgie or being **'RANDOMLY SELECTED'** to read in front of the class.

To survive, you gotta know how to blend into the background. The key to doing this is to keep a low profile. Don't talk to anyone. Don't ever look anyone in the eye – but don't look down, either. You've gotta execute the blank mannequin stare. Dress in neutral colours that camouflage with your surroundings. Don't raise your hand in class. Don't join any clubs.

I do have another reason for avoiding attention but that's a **SECRET**. (I'll tell you later. Promise. Maybe.)

Blending in does not mean not having friends, though. Life on the down-low would totally blow if I didn't have two awesome friends.

First up is

WING

emergency Frisbee

favourite shirt

lots of badges

He's a manga-reading, K-Pop-dancing captain of the Ultimate Frisbee team – who is also a total neat freak, blowing a fuse if his stuff isn't organised and tidy.

Our friendship origin story was us bonding over our shared love of kaiju monsters after Wing saw me rocking my Godzilla T-shirt on the school bus.

Next is

JOJO

Real name: Jyoti Joshi

young Scientist Club T-shirt

sensible shoes

The smartest kid in ~~school~~ the universe! A little dorky, slightly bossy, but totally **AWESOME**.

We first met when Wing and I were her lab partners in tech class, where she made a robot vacuum cleaner that could go up walls.

Wing's and my contribution was naming it 'Kevin'.

She's a mad **GENIUS** and it's safe to say that we're ALL going to be working for her someday.

CORRECTION: You're ALL going to be working for ME!

Even though I made friends with them at first because I thought they'd make an excellent shield between me and the bullies, they've really grown on me. I guess you could say we're BFFs.

Kevin!

But those were the good times. Before **THE BETRAYAL**.

Wing and JoJo are the reason I'm standing in front of the whole school.

It all started in Miss Hicks's English class, when she read us all a poem called 'The Wrong House' by a poet called A.A. Milne.

The author also wrote Winnie the Pooh!

We then had to write a poem about our homes. Which totally stumped me because I was, like, *Which one?*

Before you get the wrong idea, I'm no **MARTY MONEYBAGS** who has a regular house, a summer house and a ski lodge for the winter.

Remember that secret?

Well, here it is: **I'M A REFUGEE.**

My family came to the UK when I was very young to escape a war in our country that was making life there very **DANGEROUS**, and the UK seemed like a really nice and safe place to live.

'Why's that a secret?' you ask. 'Being a refugee is something you should be open about, right?'

Have you **HEARD** how people talk about refugees on TV? In newspapers? Or in the queue at the supermarket? Listening to them you'd think that we weren't ordinary people on a desperate journey to find somewhere safe to live. No, to some people, that is all a **DEVIOUS FIB** because they believe that refugees are all actually a sneaky team of **EVIL SUPER-SPIES** out to destroy the country from within!

So, that's why it's a secret. If I told people that I'm a refugee, I might as well strap a target to my back and alert every bully everywhere, young and old, to be mean to me.

No one can **EVER** know.

Well, except for Wing and JoJo.

They were really nice about it when I eventually told them.

'I'm so sorry that your family went through that,' said JoJo. 'But I'm glad that you're now safe, and my friend.'

'You know, all the cool superheroes are immigrants!' Wing said, counting on his fingers. 'Superman, Ms Marvel … Paddington Bear!'

They couldn't understand why I'd keep it a secret, but, like a superhero, I'm just using a **SECRET IDENTITY** to protect me and my family from harm. At least, that was the plan.

But when Miss Hicks read out that poem, it stirred up a lot of thoughts and feelings that I thought I had padlocked up in the Davy Jones's locker in my mind.

Thoughts like: *What is home?*

You see, my family has moved a lot. Since my parents, my three big sisters and I came to the UK, we've bounced between four temporary homes over five years, hoping for a permanent spot.

It's like we're a band on an **EPIC** world tour, our final stop TBC (to be confirmed).

Shackleton Academy is my third school and I've been here for almost an entire year, so it's my longest school stint so far. But there is always that nagging fear that we might move again and I'll have to start all over. **AGAIN.**

If life was a video game, I'd still be stuck on the first level.

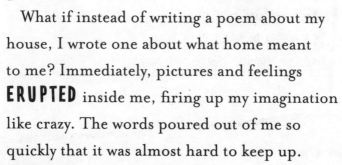

My brain pinged with a great idea.

What if instead of writing a poem about my house, I wrote one about what home meant to me? Immediately, pictures and feelings **ERUPTED** inside me, firing up my imagination like crazy. The words poured out of me so quickly that it was almost hard to keep up.

Home

Shirts and jeans and toys and books
There's so much here to pack
Fill a bag, hop in a truck
Sit quietly in the back
Say goodbye to your house
Your friends and the things you adore
Say hello to your new life
New faces and places to explore

Across the ocean, across land
We stop, knowing soon again we'll be moving
Always strange words and rules to learn
Everything is so confusing

I've learned no matter where we stay and live
Wherever we may roam
It's not a building or a place
But my family that's my home

The second I'd scribbled down the last word it felt like I'd **SNAPPED** awake from a daydream and a poem just mysteriously appeared in front of me.

Did I write it, or did it write me?

But when the bell rang and everybody started passing their poems up to the front of the class, a flurry of panicked thoughts started bouncing in my head:

What if Miss Hicks reads it and laughs?

What if she reads it out to the class and **EVERYONE** laughs?

What if everyone thinks I'm horrible like that man on the news said refugees were?

Or worse yet:

What if everyone starts calling me **'THE REFUGEE KID'** and I'm suddenly on the top of every bully's victim list?

So, I screwed up my poem, dumped it in the bin and hurried out of the door with the rest of the class.

PHEW! Embarrassment avoided!

WRONG, AGAIN!

Turns out that JoJo scooped my poem out of its early grave, read it and liked it so much that she, like a total sneak, gave it to Miss Hicks, who then gave it to the Head, who then pulled me out of geography class to see him in his office where he told me with a big smile on his face how much he liked – no, **LOVED** – my poem and that he wanted me to read it to the **ENTIRE** school!

Sorry, Kamal. I tried to stop her but her dodging techniques are UNBEATABLE!

Fast-forward to this morning and I'm standing on stage, looking out to a **PACKED** auditorium as the Head picked up the microphone.

WWWWWWRAAAAANG!

A massive ear-splitting shriek of feedback rang out.

'Kamal from Year Eight is going to read us a poem that he wrote about coming to the UK as a refugee,' said the Head. And then he stepped to the side and nudged me forward towards the microphone.

My heart was beating like crazy. It wasn't too late to do a runner. There were at least four exits in the auditorium, two of which had signs over them that read **'EMERGENCY'**, and this was definitely one of those.

Somewhere, some kids started booing.

To make things worse, I looked out at the audience and found Keisha among the wall of bored, **GLOOMY** faces. She saw that I saw her and smiled!

Normally that would have made me go all heart-eyes, but this time it just made my stage fright even worse.

Then, out of the blue, I heard my mum's voice:

Remember your Angels, Kamal. All your deeds are being recorded, so be good.

UGH! I had forgotten about those guys.

Mum was not talking about those angels up in the clouds with the big wings, the harp playing and the 'fra-la-la-la-la' chorus. No, she was talking about these *special* angels that I learned about at mosque, called the *Kiraman Katibin*.

At Quran class, they taught us that everybody has a tiny angel sitting on both shoulders. One angel is called **'RAQIB'** and the other **'ATID'**.

Raqib writes down all the good stuff that you do on their scroll, and Atid writes down all the bad stuff that you do on their scroll, and when you die, Allah, aka God, will read what the two angels have written down and decide whether you are worthy to party up in Heaven, or have an eternal bummer in Hell.

It's like the ultimate school report, but it's for your **WHOLE** life!

Nobody knows what they truly look like but, in my *imagination*, they're two tiny imams with wings and scrolls, hovering over my head and spying on everything that I do.

I guessed there was no way out of this. Walking up to the microphone, I could feel my mouth getting drier with every step. My teeth started to chatter and beads of sweat **ERUPTED** all over my face.

Then I remembered some advice an imam gave me when I kept flopping my Quran recitals:

> Relax, close your eyes and let the words flow.

So, I took a deep breath, shut my eyes and something suddenly washed over me. A deep calm.

Then – it started.

GRRROOOOOOOOWL!

Uh-oh! My stomach started churning like crazy and a hazy fog fell in front of my eyes.

'Everything OK?' asked the Head, noticing my queasiness.

Now, if I had nodded **'YES'** and legged it to the toilets, I probably would've escaped with my dignity intact, but me and smart choices go together like toothpaste and orange juice.

breakfast falafel

As soon as I opened by mouth to speak, a fountain of **VOMIT**

spewed out of it and I showered hot, lumpy puke all over the Head.

A huge gasp shot through the auditorium, followed by deathly silence.

Then somewhere, far back in the auditorium, someone let out a single **TITTER**. That was joined by others and became a snigger, which grew into a **CHUCKLE** and then a **CHORTLE**, and, in no time, it was a guffaw that exploded into a **ROAR**!

Every school kid in the auditorium was now throwing their head back, howling with laughter, tears streaming down their faces.

My form teacher, Mr Norris, rushed over
to the front of the stage and handed the Head
his handkerchief, when what the Head really
needed was a towel.

GET THIS BOY OUT OF MY SIGHT!

the Head yelled.

Mr Norris shot me a
pleading look and I scurried over
to him, just as the school bell rang.

As everyone **SCRAMBLED** out of the
auditorium to class, Wing and JoJo both came
up to me by the stage with sympathetic smiles,
but I just scowled at them. This was all their
fault! Sure, I was the **PUKER**, but none of this
would ever have happened in the first place if
JoJo hadn't fished my poem out the bin or Wing
had stopped her from giving my poem to Miss
Hicks.

31

Fortunately, I didn't have to endure their **TREACHEROUS** company for long, as Mr Norris led me away from my two-faced ex-BFFs to see the school nurse.

CHAPTER THREE

Thankfully, my time in the nurse's office was super brief but she did make me swig this icky pink concoction that had a **GROSS** tangy aftertaste that was worse than the sick I had puked out.

By the time I got to my form room, it was **UTTER CHAOS**!

Everyone was glued to their phones and the room was in a whirl of excitement.

'What's going on?' I asked.

'Everyone's checking their **POPSTOCK** ranking,' Wing answered.

'Pop *what*?'

'PopStock,' said JoJo. 'It's a new app. It has an ingenious algorithm that calculates your popularity stock based on style, athleticism, facial symmetry—'

'Basically, you can rate other people and other people can rate you,' interrupted Wing. 'You can give someone a **"COOL BUMP"** up the rankings or an **"L DROP"** down the drain, and then they get a ranking out of ten.'

'Wow! PopStock is brutal,' I said.

'Don't get sucked in, it's just a stupid app,' JoJo pointed out. 'Who cares how popular you are?'

'You're a five,' said Wing, holding up his phone, showing JoJo her ranking.

'No way!' JoJo beamed.

'I wonder what my ranking is,' I pondered out loud.

34

Wing tapped his screen a couple of times and his face fell. 'Um, you know what? JoJo is right. Who cares—'

I snatched the phone from Wing. My PopStock ranking was … **ZERO!?**

'That's the first "zero" I've seen …' Wing muttered to himself, astonished.

Me? The least popular kid in the entire school?

My ranking was lower than Barry Webster, who got his head **STUCK IN A TUBA** in the middle of a school recital and firemen had to use the jaws of life to free him!

Lower than Alana 'Gerbil Girl' Kane who **EATS NOTEBOOK PAPER**!

This had to be a mistake. Sure, I'm not the coolest kid, but I'm not a social bottom feeder. Am I?

HEY, LOOK! IT'S PUKE BOY!

Frankie Manzoli and his witless buds were chuckling at me from a couple of desks away.

And it was not just them – the whole class were smirking at me now.

Of course! How could I forget?! My embarrassing **CHUNDER-BLUNDER** at assembly must've flipped my rep from geek to freak, and now I was the **GROSSEST** kid in school!

> Better out than in, I say.

> Especially if 'out' means all over a teacher! BWAHAHA!

> Tut tut! You're as bad as them.

'Who are you gonna **SPEW** on next?' Frankie asked, making everybody chuckle.

'Leave him alone, Frankie,' said Keisha.

'Yeah, you don't want to mess around with the refu-flea,' chuckled Sid Grover. 'You'll get a rash.'

If 'Puke Boy' wasn't bad enough, now my secret's out, I'm on the bully dartboard for being a **REFUGEE** too.

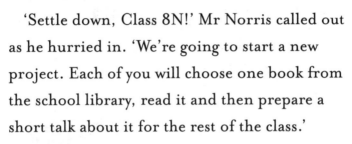

No wonder my PopStock ranking was in the sewer.

'Settle down, Class 8N!' Mr Norris called out as he hurried in. 'We're going to start a new project. Each of you will choose one book from the school library, read it and then prepare a short talk about it for the rest of the class.'

This sounded pretty easy, but I have a habit of turning **'PRETTY EASY'** into **'PRETTY DREADFUL'**. Me and homework have never really hit it off because there always seems something else far more interesting to do.

Like read a comic.

Or free a castle from ice orcs in my favourite video game.

Or make myself a quadruple decker combo sandwich.

Annoyingly, this usually ends up with me
having to do a week's worth of homework in
about half an hour.

'Let's see now,' continued Mr Norris,
scanning a teacherly eye around the classroom.

I kept my head low, as usual.

'Sid! What sort of books do you like?'
he called out.

Sid thought for a moment and said,
'Short ones, sir.'

Everyone laughed except
Mr Norris, who tutted,
UNIMPRESSED, and then carted
us all off to the school library.

Let me share another
embarrassing secret with you …
libraries **SPOOK** me out!

Mr
Norris

They are too quiet! They're like cemeteries
but with books instead of tombstones. And,
like cemeteries, if you spend too much time in
one, you begin to feel **PECULIAR** and want to
do something weird, like dance on one of the
tables, or shout **'BOGIES!'** really loudly.

38

But, mostly, libraries make me feel woozy because there are just so many books to choose from. It is choice **OVERLOAD**!

After a moment, Wing called me over to show me a book with a baboon on the cover.

JoJo, who was holding a book on steam trains, must've overheard our conversation because she leaned in.

Leaving JoJo to explain her **TERRIBLE** joke to Wing, I wandered around looking at the bookshelves, but nothing caught my eye.

Then Liam Frost came up and asked me what book I'd chosen and I said, 'Nothing yet'.

And he looked at me, all **CONFUSED**, and asked, 'What's that, then?'

I looked down and, to my surprise, there was a book in my hand!

I had **NO IDEA** how it had got there. Perhaps it fell off the shelf next to me and I caught it without realising, but when I looked over at the nearby shelf there were no gaps in its neatly lined rows of books.

See! I told you libraries were spooky.

I took a look at the book. It was called *THE CHEAT BOOK*. There was a smiley bookmark peeking out of it and, get this – I could've sworn he **WINKED** at me!

'Are you alright?' Liam asked.

Maybe I was just tired. I dropped into one of the worn library chairs while everyone else chose their books and cracked *THE CHEAT BOOK* open . . .

HELLO THERE, PAL.
FEELING LOST IN A SEA OF UNFRIENDLY CLIQUES,
BRUTAL BULLIES AND SUPER-STRICT AUTHORITY FIGURES?
CRAVING SUCCESS BUT ALLERGIC TO HARD WORK?

Woah! This book was reading my mind!

WELL, LOOK NO FURTHER!
I AM HERE TO HELP YOU. ONE LIFEHACK AT A TIME.
IT DOESN'T MATTER IF YOU'RE A BRAINIAC OR A
COMPLETE DUMMY. JUST FOLLOW THE SIMPLE STEPS LAID
OUT IN MY PAGES AND YOU'LL BE A SUCCESS.

I will?

SURE, YOU WILL.
TRUST IN THIS BOOK AND BEAT ANY OBSTACLE
IN YOUR WAY. YOU CAN AND YOU WILL!

I CAN! I WILL!

A quick flick through the book revealed it was **JAM-PACKED** with blueprints and flowchart guides showing you how to do all sorts of amazing stuff like 'HOW TO STAY UP PAST YOUR BEDTIME' and 'HOW TO MAKE THE SMELLIEST STINK BOMB'. It had the inside scoop on 'THE GOLDEN RULES OF SKIVING', 'SICK-NOTE FORGERY TIPS' and 'EASY MIRACLE CURES TO AVOID SEEING THE SCHOOL NURSE'.

It was everything that a kid could **EVER** need.

And then I had a brainwave. With this book at my disposal, I could become the **COOLEST** kid in school! That would show them all.

From **'PUKE BOY'** to **'POPULAR'** in just a few easy steps ...

This is SO UNFAIR!

CHAPTER FOUR

Before I could kick off my quest to be the best, it was time for **LUNCH**! 'Mmm! Something smells scrumptious,' JoJo sniffed, as Wing, JoJo and I walked into the cafeteria.

'Are you mad? Have you seen the half-edible concoctions that they're passing off as food today?' sighed Wing.

A kid walked past carrying a lunch tray of the sorriest-looking meal I'd **EVER** seen.

I retched a little just looking at it, and we walked a bit faster to our table.

We sat down at our usual spot in the Mutant Zone – a social wasteland of nerds, weirdos and fussy eaters.

Our spot is under a creaky ceiling fan that whips Arctic-cold air over us. I guess that's one way of being 'COOL'.

'I made my own lunch today,' said Wing. He took a bulging, brown paper bag out of his backpack and pulled out from it the most epic sandwich of all time. 'I call this the Super Deluxe, Quadruple Decker, Foot-Tall, WING-WICH!' he continued, proudly.

The sight of this edible monstrosity got our whole table's attention.

'It's a MASTERPIECE!' squeaked a tiny Year Seven boy in awe. 'Mind if I have a bite?'

'Sure, what's one bite?' replied Wing, graciously.

Famous last words – because when this tiny boy opened his minuscule gob for a bite, his jaw kept dropping lower and lower, and then MUNCHED half of Wing's giant sandwich in one loud CHOMP.

45

Wing sniffed sadly, holding what was left of his Wing-wich.

'You're welcome to a slice of my **HELLA HEALTHY** and totally tasty chickpea and beetroot quiche,' offered JoJo, proudly presenting her plate of putrid pink pastry to Wing like she was a baking-show contestant.

'Uh. No, thanks,' said Wing. 'What about you, Kamal? What've you got?'

'Sorry, no sharing today. My mum made my favourite,' I gloated, popping open my food flask to pour out Mum's next level *digaag qumbe* into a bowl.

I closed my eyes and inhaled its aroma. **MMM!** Earthy. Spicy.

Rice

yoghurt coconut chicken

Coriander

Banana

PEEEEEE-YEW! WHAT'S THAT SMELL?

I opened my eyes and found myself surrounded by a small crowd, all holding their noses and gawping at my lunch.

'Whatchu eating, Puke Boy? Vomit soup?'

'Look! There's something **FLOATING** in it!'

'It's a … banana—? In a stew? Gross!'

OK, so, Somali food can be a little … **DIFFERENT**. A banana in the middle of a stew is unusual (and delicious), but it's not like British food doesn't have its share of culinary oddities. Might I present …

Haggis
(a sheep's heart and liver cooked in an animal's stomach!)

Black Pudding
(made of blood!)

And don't get me started on jellied eels!

Yet, here I was being yucked at!

My face began to burn with embarrassment.
I wanted to tell them all to **SHOVE OFF** but every
time I opened my mouth no words came out as
the sound of their laughter grew.

From the corner of my eye, I could see Wing
getting more and more cross, until he sprang up
from his seat, **EXPLODING** like a volcano.

'What're you laughing at, Fred?' he
yelled, pointing at one of the boys.
'Didn't you have baked-bean pizzas at
your birthday?'

There was a loud guffaw and Wing turned
on a boy with his finger in his nose. 'And you!
I don't think eating your bogies counts as your
five-a-day,' he sneered.

The cloud of unwanted attention now away
from me, I picked up my spoon, ready to
chow down on my favourite meal.

If things had ended like this then it
would've been **PERFECT**.

But then life threw another JoJo-sized
wrench into my already clunker of a day.

SEVEN THINGS HAPPENED NEXT...

Then someone, somewhere, yelled, **'FOOD FIGHT!'** and the entire cafeteria exploded into a free-for-all flurry of tossed edibles.

Kids were standing on chairs and lobbing food. Klaus, the huge, hulking, Austrian exchange student, used his chair as a shield and was heard ordering everyone at his table: 'If it breathes, we splat it!'

It was **MAYHEM**! Total **MADNESS**!

When it had just reached peak pandemonium, a loud whistle shrilled across the cafeteria, freezing everyone to the spot.

The Head stood at the cafeteria entrance, whistle in hand. A Fuming Maroon on the Temper Scale.

As he surveyed the **MONSTROUS MESS**, he wasn't getting any calmer.

Mashed potatoes dripped down the walls. Soup puddles, baked beans and lumps of corned beef lay in blobs on the floor. Bits of spaghetti dangled from the ceiling fans.

If looks could kill, we'd all be in the morgue.

WHAT IS THE MEEEEEEEANING OF ALL THIS?

No one answered.

Everyone knows that there's no meaning to a food fight other than **FUN**, but adults (sorrowful creatures that have had all the fun sucked out of them when they stopped being kids) love to ask **SILLY** questions. Stuff like:

As a kid, what you're supposed to do when an adult asks you a silly question like that is to let it hang in the air and wait for them to calm down a bit, but little Milly Hobbs clearly didn't get the memo.

'Um, it's a food fight, sir.'

This only made the Head angrier.

'I KNOW THAT! WHO STARTED IT?'

They say that there's honour among thieves, but school kids? Not on your life! Everyone **POINTED** at our table just as Wing, JoJo and I crawled out from under it.

'KAMAL! That's twice today you've created a **HORRIBLE** mess!' roared the Head. 'And this time, you have two partners in crime.'

He called us over. Wing gave me a look that said 'Here we go again' but JoJo looked mortified. She had **NEVER** been in trouble before.

Getting a closer look at her, the Head couldn't believe his eyes. 'Jyoti Joshi? Our little gem of STEM? What are you doing hanging with these two upstarts?'

'Somebody's gotta look out for them,' JoJo laughed nervously.

Look out for us? She started this mess!

'Seeing that you're our star pupil, I'll let you off with a warning just this once, Jyoti, but **DON'T** let me catch you again,' threatened the Head.

'Girl Guide's honour,' said JoJo, doing a three-finger salute.

'As for you two troublemakers,' growled the Head, fixing Wing and me in his mean sights. 'First you're going to clean up this mess. And I mean **ALL OF IT**! I want to be able to see my reflection in the floor. And then I want to see both of you in my office. Do I make myself clear?'

'YES, SIR!' we both barked.

As Wing and I walked over to the dinner ladies who handed us mops and buckets, I could hear kids whispering 'Legends!' and 'Best food fight ever!'

Maybe I'd finally shaken off the shackles of Puke Boy to become the Food Fight Kid?

The atmosphere outside the Head's office was thick with **DREAD**.

It wasn't just my nerves: from the walls that were painted a cheerless eggshell to the **TEDIOUS** ticking of the clock above our heads, which made me want to pull my ears off, it's like this place was designed to be grim and hopeless to soften you up for the punishment to come.

Getting scolded by the Head was just half of my problems. When Mum and Dad found out that I had gotten myself into trouble not once but **TWICE** in one day, I would be done for. No video games. No comics. Double chores.

Unless …

Whilst Wing was caught up in his own worry spiral, I snuck out *THE CHEAT BOOK* from my school bag. As soon as I set it on my lap, the book fell open on a page that read:

SO, YOU'VE FOUND YOURSELF
IN THE PRINCIPAL'S OFFICE?

Whoa! That was creepy...

UH-OH! BEING SENT TO THE PRINCIPAL'S OFFICE IS THE
SECOND WORST PLACE IN SCHOOL TO BE (SEE: EXAMS).
IF YOU DON'T GO IN WITH A PLAN, YOU'VE MOST LIKELY
DOOMED YOURSELF TO A DETENTION,
OR, AT WORST, EXPULSION.
BUT DON'T YOU WORRY, BUDDY, BECAUSE
I'VE GOT MORE THAN ONE STRATEGY TO HELP GET
YOU OFF SCOT-FREE.

TO LEAVE THE
PRINCIPAL'S OFFICE ALIVE
TIP #1
LOOKS ARE IMPORTANT. TRY NOT TO LOOK GUILTY.
1. IF YOU'RE TOO ANGELIC, YOU'RE GUILTY AS SIN.
2. IF YOU'RE A LITTLE NERVOUS, YOU'RE SAFE.

Wing and I were called into the Head's gloomy
office and were told to sit down on the plastic
interrogation chairs in front of his desk.

The Head grinned at us behind steepled
fingers like a super-villain.

56

After glaring at us for an uncomfortable second, the Head, like a deranged Jack-in-the-box, sprang up on his feet and leaned so far over his desk that his now angry purple, pulsating head hovered uncomfortably in our personal space, and eyeball-to-eyeball with us, he roared: **'PANDEMONIUM!'**

I swallowed hard, squirming nervously in my butt-numbing chair.

'Do you know what that word means?' he asked us.

TIP #2

IF THE PRINCIPAL QUIZZES YOU OR ACCUSES YOU OF SOMETHING, PRETEND TO BE SO SHOCKED THAT YOU'RE TEMPORARILY SPEECHLESS. THIS WILL BUY YOU SOME TIME WHILE YOU THINK OF AN ANSWER.

So, I stared at the Head, boggle-eyed and with my mouth hanging open, trying my best to look like the village **IDIOT** while I wracked my brain for the answer.

Pandemonium means a state of wild and noisy disorder or confusion, sir.

Now my mouth hung open in **SHOCK** for real. How on earth did Wing know that?

'That's actually correct, young man,' the Head stammered in surprise.

'Wing, sir. My name is Wing.'

'New boy, huh?'

'No, sir,' Wing replied.

'Never seen you before in my life,' the Head admitted. 'But with word knowledge like that, why aren't you in the Spelling Squad? We've got a big game next week against the Ipswich Idioms.'

'Oh, no, I'm rubbish with words, sir. But I used to play a lot of *Pandemonium*! You know – the video game?'

The Head made a **YUCK** face at the mention of 'video game' and sat back down in his chair. 'The word "pandemonium",' he explained, 'was the name of the capital city of Hell, which is fitting because you two caused all **HELL** to break loose today in MY cafeteria! I haven't seen such terrible behaviour in my **ENTIRE** life!'

Which I found hard to believe because the Head was a fossil.

TIP #3
STILL IN TROUBLE, EH? YEESH! OK, NOT TO WORRY.
NEXT STEP: DENY EVERYTHING.
BLAME SOMEONE ELSE.
STICK TO YOUR STORY. LIE LIKE CRAZY.
IF YOU PULL THIS OFF, NOT ONLY
WILL IT SAVE YOUR NECK
BUT YOU SHOULD CONSIDER A CAREER IN POLITICS.

'No! No, sir. We had absolutely nothing to do with it. Me? In a food fight? I'm Muslim, sir. Wasting food is **HARAM**! Besides, what if a stray bacon roll got in my mouth?'

The Head chuckled like he didn't believe a word but then something strange happened. He gave me a **WEIRD** look. It was the same look that Wing made every time he handed over his favourite card after I beat him in a Pokémon battle. The look of ... **DEFEAT**?!

'Just before you came in here, it was brought to my attention that you two may *not* have entirely caused this,' sighed the Head.

Wing and I quickly glanced at each other, stunned.

'One of the prefects informed me that there is strong evidence to suggest that the **REAL CULPRIT** is still at large, but I was hoping you two would confess,' said the Head. 'No matter, I'll have the slippery scamp caught by the final bell.'

The Head then pulled out two envelopes from the inside pocket of his blazer jacket.

'I had letters typed for your parents,' the Head continued, with a bitter smile.

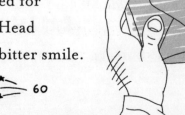

'You're safe for now but one false move ... one more projectile – vomit, food or otherwise – and I'm hand-delivering these to your parents!'

CRUMBS! If my parents ever read that letter, they'd ship me back to Somalia, all alone!

You're here for good grades.

Not naughty escapades.

I can't let that happen! I need a 'worst-case scenario' plan!

Now, Dad drives a bus all day, which means the chances of him being around to pick up the letter are very slim. That leaves Mum. The thing is, Mum's English isn't great, so when Dad's not around, my sisters and I translate letters for her. If I stay **CLOSE** to Mum and manage to grab the letter before my sisters do (they would

looooove to read a bad school letter about me)
then I can **'TRANSLATE'** the letter myself and
edit out the bad bits.

And maybe I could even slip in a few good
comments here and there ...

Dear Parent,

We are ~~sorry~~ proud to inform
you that Kamal ~~has~~
~~detention for his poor~~
~~behaviour.~~
is the BEST STUDENT in
Shackleton Academy HISTORY!
So, as a reward we are giving
him the rest of the school year
off to play video games.

This plan is way too **RISKY**. It relies on too many things going right.

There was no way out of this. I had to make sure I didn't get in trouble again, or I'd be **TOAST**.

Wing and I lowered our heads and promised not to step out of line. Clearly not entirely convinced by our answers, the Head sent us off to class. Wing and I could not believe our ears — we'd got away with it!

Just as I opened the door for us to leave, the Head yelled, 'Watch your step! I have my **EYES** on you **BOTH**!'

'What just happened?' a bewildered Wing asked, outside the Head's office.

I shrugged, trying to hold back a massive smile.

Oh, I forgot to mention: *THE CHEAT BOOK* had a tip #0.

TIP #0

CREATE A RUMOUR. IF YOU CAN, MAKE UP TWO BUT NO MORE. IF IT CATCHES ON, IT WILL SEED DOUBT IN EVERYBODY'S MIND ABOUT WHAT ACTUALLY HAPPENED AND CAN, IF DONE WELL, GET YOU OFF THE HOOK.

As much as it would've been awesome to have been known as the outlaw heroes who kickstarted the most **EPIC** food fight that Shackleton Academy had ever seen, it wasn't worth getting into trouble with my parents.

So, I took *THE CHEAT BOOK*'s advice and found Floss the Goss and told her that the real culprits of the food fight were actually the dinner ladies, who, having had enough of the constant mickey-taking of their cooking, had finally taken their **REVENGE** by throwing it back in our faces. Literally.

SCHOOL GOSSIP

As expected, in no time, the dinner-lady revolt was all anyone could talk about. So that meant it would have reached the ears of Humphrey Jenkins, the resident **SNITCH** and All-Seeing Spy for the Head – who was also his dad! What I didn't expect, though, were all the **OTHER** rumours that sprang up.

I reckon the E numbers in the processed food triggered a case of mass hysteria.

Actually, Hamzah in Year 10 started the food fight because Zak in Year 11 told him he was crap at football.

He said wot? I wasn't even in there, I was at the dentist! And I'm the BEST at football in the entire school ...

There was even one rumour that claimed there was no food fight at all, and that it was actually a case of **SPONTANEOUS COMBUSTION** of foodstuffs!

Hehe, that one may have been me.

Like *THE CHEAT BOOK* promised, Wing and I were off scot-free. But I could not shake the feeling of the watchful eye of the Head everywhere I went …

ONE!? I tricked myself out of detention! I should be at least a THREE.

CHAPTER FIVE

When I got home from school, I could smell that Mum was cooking spicy baked mackerel. Somali translation: *kalluun duban*.

I hate *kalluun duban*, but I couldn't eat anyway because I had **BIGGER** FISH TO FRY.

THE CHEAT BOOK WORKS!

I, Mr Stay-in-the-Background-and-Never-Make-a-Peep, got into the most epic trouble (through no fault of my own, of course!) and was saved by ... a book?!

This was **BIG**! This was **MEGA**! This was the most outrageous thing in the history of **OUTRAGEOUS** things!

My head was swimming with fantasies of where this book could take me.

I could be top of **EVERY** class!

The life of the party!

Prefect! *No.* Head Student!

No, I should dream bigger. I could use it to **WIN** at school!

Sounds funny – 'win at school' – doesn't it? Like it's a game. But school *IS* a game. **LITERALLY**. One we play to earn good grades, and now with the PopStock app, popularity points.

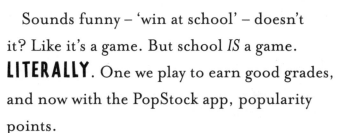

I should have celebrated with a toasted s'mores milkshake, but my mind was suddenly flooded with whys.

The only answer I could come up with was

MAYBE IT WAS A GIFT, like Excalibur or

Thor's hammer.

A magical item that finds the people that need

it most.

As a refugee, I've been through a lot. I've been

shuffled around different schools like a pack of

cards. Forever the new kid, always a **DORK**.

But *THE CHEAT BOOK* could change all that. I

could finally be …

'How was school, kids?' Mum asked, flopping a slice of *kalluun duban* on to our plates.

'At lunchtime, Kamal took "playing with your food" to a whole new level. Didn't you, bro?' smirked my sister, Yasmin, setting my other sisters off cackling like witches.

I have **THREE** sisters:

yasmin AKA the GLAM one and also the eldest

Samira AKA the BRAINY one

Halima AKA the GOTH one

If living with them wasn't bad enough, having them go to the same school as me and knowing my **EVERY** move was worse than being haunted.

Like wolves, they move as a pack, tripling their power to irritate and annoy their prey (ME) by forming into a single creature that I call ...

THE SISTER BEAST!

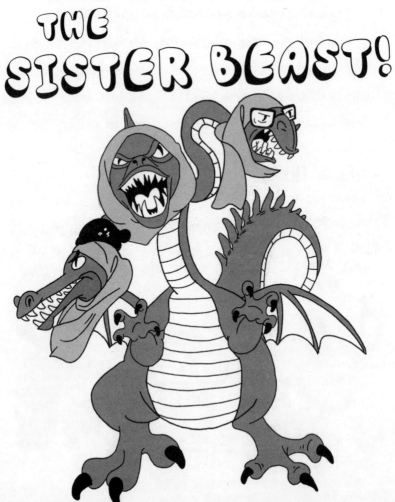

I scowled at Yasmin, which only made my sisters chuckle more.

'Congrats on finally getting some bumps on PopStock,' said Samira.

'Yeah, you're no longer the **BIGGEST** loser. Just a **REGULAR** loser,' added Halima.

'Takes one to know one,' I snapped back.

'You wish!' sneered Samira. And, as if on cue, my sisters held up their phones and showed off their PopStock rankings.

Like the **DEVIL**!

Actually, The Devil doesn't have a number in Islam, so relax.

But 666 might just be the number of bad deeds you have.

How was this real?!

How were **THEY** more popular than **ME**?

I felt like I'd been teleported to a strange, backwards universe where cats chased dogs and dad jokes were funny.

What cruel and unfair system was this? It only made me even more determined to win more points and **SMASH** it!

After dinner, I ran up to my room and grabbed *THE CHEAT BOOK* out my backpack.

When I'd first used it, I'd put the book on my lap and it had miraculously fallen open on the page that I needed.

I tried that again but this time it just lay on my lap, closed. So, I did something kinda ridiculous.

'Hey, *CHEAT BOOK*. Uh, I hope you're … good? Um, I was just wondering, could you help me get more **"COOL BUMPS"** on PopStock?'

Of course, nothing happened. I was talking to a book!

But then … like a spell book in a cartoon, *THE CHEAT BOOK* flipped itself open and its pages began to flick wildly until it stopped on a specific page.

'FROM HOT MESS TO BEST DRESSED'
YOUR QUICKEST FIX IS A TOTAL STYLE REMIX.

WHOA! There it was again. That same chill down my spine from when I used it the first time. A shiver of excitement and fear. But there was no time for any of that now, because it was makeover time.

Seeing that my **GEEKTASTIC** style was sinking my score, my first destination was my parents' room and to Dad's side of the wardrobe. Luckily, he was still at work, driving his bus.

I pushed past all his smart work clothes and dived into the back of the wardrobe to see what flashy gear he had hiding.

Dad doesn't rock the **'NORMAL'** dad attire, but instead likes to kick it Somali and wear a linen shirt, a sarong-like wrap called a *macawiis* and an embroidered cap called a *koofyad*.

All of which are not **COOL KID FRIENDLY**. But he does own a pair of cool shades that *THE CHEAT BOOK* said was essential.

So, I cycled over to the charity shop around the corner and with the **PUNY SAVINGS** in my money jar managed to put together an outfit that ticked all the boxes.

I took a look in the mirror and saw a whole new Kamal twinkling at me. Was that a good thing? I couldn't tell, but I was going to trust *THE CHEAT BOOK.*

'What's happened to your ... *everything*?!'

My sisters were all gawping at me at the bus stop like I had dropped in from another planet. Which I had. **PLANET COOL. POPULATION: ME!**

'Is that one of my clip-on earrings **IN** your **NOSE**?!' cried Yasmin.

'Want it back?' I asked, taking the nose ring out and offering it to her.

'EW! KEEP IT!' screamed Yasmin, pushing my hand away.

I DON'T WANT YOUR ICKY NOSTRIL GERMS!

'You seem taller,' said Samira, looking me up and down suspiciously.

'Half an inch,' I smiled. 'It's called a growth spurt, loser.'

'That's not how that works!' snapped Samira. 'You haven't even hit puberty!'

'What can I say? I'm an early starter.' I shrugged.

Actually, I'm a head-starter thanks to *THE CHEAT BOOK*.

IF YOU'RE A PIPSQUEAK,
FIND WAYS TO PROJECT YOURSELF.
SUGGESTIONS:
TRY A BIGGER HAIRSTYLE OR SHOE LIFTS.

I had slipped two door stoppers in the heels of my socks.

'There's only one spurt coming out of you,' scoffed Halima, and mimed throwing up.

Even the teasing from my sisters couldn't bring me down. I had a brand-new **LOOK** and I couldn't wait for everyone at school to see.

When I arrived at school, I strutted through the front gates and braced myself for **SUPERSTARDOM**.

Drumroll, please …
SILENCE.

No cheering. No chanting. No being mobbed for selfies. Just … nothing. A few of the older kids side-eyed me but were obviously too intimidated by my **AWESOMENESS** to approach me.

I spotted Wing and JoJo sitting at one of the picnic benches by the playground and made a beeline over to them, **ZIGZAGGING** through the sea of other school kids.

''Sup, guys?' I said, lowering my sunglasses
and giving them a wink.

Wing and JoJo just stared at me. Stunned by
my **BRILLIANCE**, no doubt.

'Um, interesting outfit ...' said JoJo.

'Do you like it? I'm dressed for PopStock
success,' I replied, sprawling out on the bench
beside them.

'More like dressed for Halloween,' Wing
chortled. He reached out and felt the sleeve of
my shirt. 'Is this **100 PER CENT COTTON**?' he
asked. 'Because it should be
100 PER CENT FORGOTTEN.'

'That's not nice, Wing,' tutted JoJo.

'Laugh it up,' I said to Wing, shrugging my
backpack off my shoulders. 'Because soon my
ranking will **ROCKET** and I'm going to leave you
both in the dust.' I pulled out *THE CHEAT BOOK*
from my backpack and plonked it on the picnic
table.

'What's with the big old dusty tome, Gandalf?'
Wing grinned.

I ignored him and leaned forward. 'Hey, *CHEAT BOOK*,' I whispered. 'How do I trade my lunch for something better?'

JoJo and Wing shared a look as if to say, 'Has Kamal gone crazy?'

As expected, *THE CHEAT BOOK* flipped itself open on the picnic table and its pages began to turn as if a wind had blown across them. Almost as quickly as it had begun, the pages stopped turning on this chapter:

'FROM CRUMMY TO YUMMY:
THE SCHOOL-LUNCH BARTERING GUIDE'

'OH-EM-GEE! You really **ARE** a wizard!' gasped Wing. 'Please tell me that you're a magical **CHOSEN ONE** who's about to drag us all off on an epic fantasy adventure rated PG for mild peril.'

'Not likely,' huffed JoJo. 'It's obviously some sort of voice-activated encyclopaedia.'

'You're close, JoJo.' I smiled. 'It's actually a *CHEAT BOOK*.'

'A what?' Wing and JoJo said together.

'It's a handbook full of tips and tricks to help you come out on top of any sticky situation,' I replied.

'That's so sick!' exclaimed Wing, who was now flicking through its pages. 'An entire book of **LIFE HACKS**!'

JoJo did not look convinced. 'Guys, *"CHEAT BOOK"* doesn't sound very honest. Sounds like a lot of trouble, if you ask me.'

Wing and I groaned.

'It's actually been the opposite,' I explained. 'Without it, me and Wing would be in **DETENTION** until we're thirty. Besides, I'm done following the rules. I did that and look where it got me – a **ZERO** rating. You're now seeing Kamal 2.0. I do what I want, when I want, and I answer to no—'

'OI! PUKE HEAD!'

UH-OH! Towering right behind me was Neville Sykes, the biggest bully in school.

And standing on either side of him were his two minions, Sid and Knuckles.

This was bad. Everybody calls Neville 'the Ogre' because he's the size of four regular-sized bullies, and **FOUR TIMES AS MEAN**.

He was a **MONSTER**, and he had set his sights on **ME**!

OK, if I don't look back, he might leave me alone. I mean, he might not even be talking to me.

WeLL done for avoiding trouble.

UGH! This Kid is no fun.

'No one told us it was **'DRESS UP LIKE A CLOWN DAY'**,' sneered Sid, with a gap-toothed grin.

I opened my mouth to say something, but nothing came out. Why couldn't I talk? My throat had gone dry all of a sudden.

'**URGH!** What is up with your hair? It **REEKS**!' asked Knuckles, holding his nose.

'Oh, it's coconut oil,' I told him.

'Makes sense when your head looks like a coconut!' snorted Knuckles, cracking up his mates.

The Ogre, a wicked glint in his eye, turned to Sid, and commanded: '**BRING OUT THE TING!**'

Oh, no! Not '**THE TING**'! Anything but the ... Wait, what's '**THE TING**'?

Sid took out a furry bathroom mat from his messenger bag and laid it out on the ground in front of me, sniggering.

With a cruel smirk, the Ogre put on a pair of bike gloves that had **ALUMINIUM FOIL** taped on them and then took his shoes off, revealing socks that had more holes than old Swiss cheese and smelt just as bad. With bated breath I watched him as he stepped on the furry bathroom mat and started to **SHUFFLE** his feet superfast.

What in the world was he doing?!

I was about to find out, as the Ogre had stopped shuffling and lunged towards me with his finger and **ZAP!** **'AAARGGGH!'** I screamed.

The Ogre and his cronies burst out laughing.

'I don't get it. What's happening?' asked Wing.

'The Ogre zapped Kamal,' replied JoJo.

'How?' asked Wing.

'When his feet rubbed the carpet, he built up a charge of static electricity, and touched Kamal, giving him a shock.'

ZAP!
ZAP!
ZAP!

The Ogre had whipped up quite a crowd. A gaggle of laughter **ERUPTED** between every shock.

This was terrible! This **GOOFY BUG-ZAPPER** was turning me into the joke of the entire school. Again. I could feel my PopStock rating **PLUMMETING** back to zero.

I had to do something, but what?

I felt a rumbling. It wasn't in my stomach this time, but my guts.

ZAP! That one hurt! My sunglasses fell off my head and hit the ground.

The Ogre **LUNGED** at me, static crackling across his pointed finger. I braced myself for another stinging shock but ...

All those static shocks had been wreaking havoc on my digestion, causing the gas in my guts to bubble out and release its **GASSY PRISONERS** into the open and, by the smell of them, they must've all been doing hard time!

The **NOXIOUS, EGGY PLUMES** sent the crowd around us scurrying and spluttering off in many directions.

The smell only made the Ogre **MORE** angry and he lunged at me with furious eyes – but slipped and fell.

I spotted something shiny crushed under him: sunglasses! The Ogre must've tripped over them. My outfit had saved me. Which meant, *THE CHEAT BOOK* had saved me once again!

Sid and Knuckles helped lift the Ogre up just as the school bell went. 'This isn't over, Puke Boy. Watch, after school.'

GULP.

Seconds after the bullies scampered off, my phone **PINGED**. I had received a calendar event invite on my phone from the Ogre:

THE BIG FIGHT INVITATION

FROM: Neville 'The Ogre' Sykes
DAY: TODAY
TIME: 3:00PM to 3:01PM
LOCATION: School Field

Accept   Decline

Say what you want about Neville, but for a nitwit bully, the boy sure was organised.

It was then that I noticed it.

Everyone in the playground was frozen and staring at me as I headed for class. It was even worse inside school. The corridors – usually noisy and crammed with everyone pushing and shoving each other – were now silent as the grave. A crowd of school kids parted for me, Wing and JoJo as we walked through.

'DEAD MAN WALKING!' someone yelled. And that was exactly what it felt like.

'At least we can get to class quicker,' said JoJo, trying to lighten the mood.

'Can't you see all their faces?' I fretted. 'I'm a **GONER**!'

'Hey, we're all gonna go sometime,' Wing shrugged, putting his arm around my shoulder. 'You're just going sooner.'

JoJo shoved Wing aside and put a reassuring hand on my arm. 'We should go and tell the principal what's going on. I'm sure he'll fix it.'

'NO WAY!' I cried. 'I'm already on the Head's watch list after the food fight and if he finds out about the fight, he'll send a letter to my parents and then I'll be in **REAL** trouble.

No, I'm going to handle this on my own.'

'What's the plan, then?'

'I'll hide,' I answered. 'Neville can't fight what he can't see.'

'Hide? What, until graduation?' Wing laughed.

'I didn't say that it was a good plan.'

'Well, you're not the first kid to hide from the Ogre. I bet he knows every hiding spot in school.'

Wing was right. Between the Ogre and his **HENCHMEN**, I'd be hunted down and pummelled into **SOUR-BRO PIZZA** in no time. I had to come up with a better plan.

Usually, the school day feels **NEVER-ENDING** until three o'clock, but I was so busy imagining escape plans that time flew by and before I knew it, it was the last lesson of the day. I guess fear has a way of making the day go faster.

ESCAPE PLAN #1
Tunnel Out!

ESCAPE PLAN #2
Camouflage

But when I sat down in my creaky chair
for history class, I realised that I had an even
SCARIER problem on my plate than the Ogre.

I had been so busy with my makeover that I
had forgotten to do my history homework for
the **MEANEST** TEACHER in the whole school!

CHAPTER SIX

Unluckily for me, Wing and JoJo weren't in my history class, so copying their homework wasn't an option.

I was **TOAST**.

Any other teacher would be content with a classic …

I left my homework on the bus, sir.

Or, if you're really in a jam …

There was a blackout and I had to burn my homework for light, miss.

93

That's because most teachers are eager to play the 'I won't mess with you, if you don't bug me' game.

But, not Ms Drood.

Ms Drood is the meanest teacher in the history of mean teachers.

She is **THE DEVIL**!

No, wait – not the Devil.

DROOD-ZILLA!

She was so mean, I was sure she had a second job at the London Dungeon, dreaming up frightening new methods of **TORTURE**.

Giving out detentions was her favourite thing.

Wait! That was perfect!

Detention would get me out of having to face the Ogre after school!

94

But how would I get a detention? Surely it couldn't be too hard with Ms Drood. Especially since I had forgotten my homework. But no, I couldn't risk it.

Maybe *THE CHEAT BOOK* could help …

ARE YOU SURE?
ACTING UP COULD ALSO EASILY BACKFIRE
AND GET YOU SUSPENDED, OR WORSE, EXPELLED!

Hmm, maybe just some light pranking?

It was personal history week, so for that day's history lesson we all had to draw a family tree. I was finished **WAAAAY** before anyone else. That's because everyone else was drawing these ginormous trees with lots of branches of grandparents, aunts, uncles and cousins, whilst my family tree looked more like a sapling.

That was because my family had left everyone else behind when we came to the UK and my parents never really spoke about them. Maybe because it hurt to. I was a toddler when we left Somalia, so I couldn't really remember anyone specific – just a **BLURRY** slideshow of smiling faces.

When I had finished my family tree, I got busy on my genius plan.

MISSION GET DETENTION AND **ESCAPE THE OGRE** was a go.

Let the games begin!

TIP #1:
BE ANNOYINGLY CURIOUS.

I started small by asking Ms Drood distracting questions every time she spoke, like:

MS, could you repeat that? No, not that bit, the bit before that.

MS, spell that out for me, please?

But Ms Drood wasn't fazed by my badgering at all. In fact, she **LOVED** it!?

TIP #2:
ASK QUESTIONS THAT HAVE NOTHING
TO DO WITH ANYTHING.

Time to move on to the silly questions, like:

MS, how do islands not float away?

MS, why do meteors always land in craters?

MS, can I go see the school nurse? I think sitting next to the radiator is giving me radiation poisoning?

The class was in hysterics, but Ms Drood only gave me an odd look. Since I had never acted up in class before, maybe she thought radiation poisoning **HAD** got to me.

This was going to be tough. It was time to switch gears.

TIP #3:

WEAPONISED VENTRILOQUISM.
FRY THEIR OLD-PERSON BRAIN BY
'THROWING' YOUR VOICE.

I started making little **MEOWING** noises without moving my lips.

This made the whole class giggle except Ms Drood, whose **BEADY** eyes searched every kid's face but, to my dismay, she couldn't find the phantom meow-er because her hearing wasn't the sharpest.

Who knew that getting into trouble would be so **HARD**?!

Ms Drood asked everyone to put their textbooks down.

She then asked if anyone would like to volunteer to read their homework out to the rest of class.

THIS WAS MY **FINAL CHANCE.** I would make up some ridiculous excuse and that would get me detention for sure.

Of course it helped that I had actually forgotten to do my homework ...

To nobody's surprise, there were **ZERO** volunteers. This wasn't because everyone was shy. My class is jam-packed with show-offs and windbags. No, this was because Ms Drood had turned class reading into the most toe-curling public **HUMILIATION**, where she would give a running commentary and grade you in front of the whole class at the end.

I got my lie ready. I needed something really ridiculous—

My homework was abducted by aliens!

Or, it was so good my mum wanted to display it on the fridge.

'If it helps,' Ms Drood frowned, 'I've been tasked with umpiring this evening's tennis match on account of Mrs Singh's flu, which means no detention.'

Oh, no.

'Still no volunteers? Gutless, as ever,' scorned Ms Drood. And then she *smiled*. It was a joyless, sinister grin that sent a shiver down everyone's spines. 'Looks like I'm going to have to pick someone,' she declared. 'But let's spice things up. Since I can't give you detention today, if your report is really bad, I'll send a letter to your parents!'

NoOooOooOooOo.

The only thing worse than getting pounded to mush by the Ogre was getting into trouble with my parents. They knew how to make my life a **LIVING HELL**!

I could feel Ms Drood's searchlight glare roving across the classroom, hunting for a victim. My only hope now was *THE CHEAT BOOK*.

'Hey, *CHEAT BOOK*,' I whispered, 'how do I not get picked to read in class?' *THE CHEAT BOOK* quietly turned to a new page.

HOW TO NOT GET PICKED IN CLASS
TO GET YOURSELF OFF THE HOOK,
IT'S ALL ABOUT HOW YOU LOOK.

TIP #1:

PUT ON A SLEEPY SMILE. THIS WILL HOPEFULLY MAKE
YOUR TEACHER IMMEDIATELY DOUBT THAT YOU'LL HAVE
ANYTHING USEFUL TO CONTRIBUTE.

Spacing out was easy. I imagined myself snuggled up in my big duvet with my fluffy cat, Rumi, and I instantly started to drift off with a dopey grin on my face.

'**KAMAL**,' called Ms Drood, making me jolt up in my seat. 'You've been quite the chatterbox today. How about sharing your inevitably fascinating work with the class?'

I was busted. There were now only two choices: sink or swim.

I hid *THE CHEAT BOOK* inside my ring binder and walked to the front of the class.

Next to me, Ms Drood sat perched on the end of her desk, wearing a big, satisfied grin.

TIP #1:

MAKE SOMETHING UP.

(THAT WAY NO ONE CAN

CHECK YOU FOR ACCURACY.)

'Angus McSporran,' I said, maybe a bit too loudly, 'was a Scottish outlaw who I learned about in a **SUPER-RARE** book called *Heroes of the Highland*.'

'Oh?' interrupted Ms Drood. 'As a Scot myself, I'm unfamiliar with the McSporran clan.'

'They're an extinct clan,' I lied. 'I believe they perished in the Battle of, uh, Balamory.'

TIP #2:

MENTION ALL THE BORING

RESEARCH YOU DID.

(TEACHERS ARE ALWAYS IMPRESSED BY THIS.)

'The *Heroes of the Highland* is one thousand pages long.'

'You read the **ENTIRE** thing over a weekend?' wondered Ms Drood.

'No. I listened to the audio book at ten times the usual speed!' I lied again.

TIP #3:
THROW IN A TEACHER COMPLIMENT.

'Angus was incredibly talented because he had a terrific teacher who taught him everything he knew,' I said, winking at Ms Drood. She just glared.

TIP #4:
USE BIG WORDS GENEROUSLY AND ALWAYS INCLUDE A MORAL.

'Angus showed that equity was a principle that humanity should safeguard unremittingly.'

'Wow! Somebody ate a thesaurus for breakfast!' joked Ms Drood, making the class giggle.

'Thanks for listening and let me leave you with some advice from the great Angus – "Mony a mickle maks a muckle".'

Everyone politely clapped, looking a little **BAFFLED** by what they'd heard.

'Well, that was interesting,' said Ms Drood, sarcastically. 'You have certainly mastered the skill of saying a lot without actually saying anything at all. That non-report deserves a plain old "D". You may sit down.'

I MADE IT! I SURVIVED!

Ms Drood looked really confused as to why I was so over the moon after being given such a low grade, but my joy was short-lived because I remembered that even though I might've survived one threat, another one still loomed on the horizon: **THE OGRE.**

Wait! Of course! Why hadn't I thought of this sooner?

'Hey, *CHEAT BOOK*. How do I get out of a bully beatdown?'

FINALLY! I'VE BEEN WAITING FOR YOU TO ASK!
BESIDES
A) TELLING A TEACHER (THIS IS THE SENSIBLE OPTION BUT COULD MAKE YOU A 'TATTLETALE');
OR
B) EMIGRATING TO TIMBUKTU (EXPENSIVE);
OR
C) FAKING YOUR OWN DEATH (COMPLICATED),
YOU ARE LEFT WITH ONLY TWO OTHER PAIN-FREE OPTIONS: EVASION AND ESCAPE.

TIP #1:

NEVER BE MORE THAN 1 METRE AWAY FROM A BULLY-FREE ZONE (A CLASSROOM, A PREFECT, A TEACHER).

TIP #2:

TAPE A COUPLE OF MINI ROCKETS TO THE SIDES OF A BACKPACK AND YOU'VE GOT A JETPACK TO SPEED PAST YOUR BULLY.

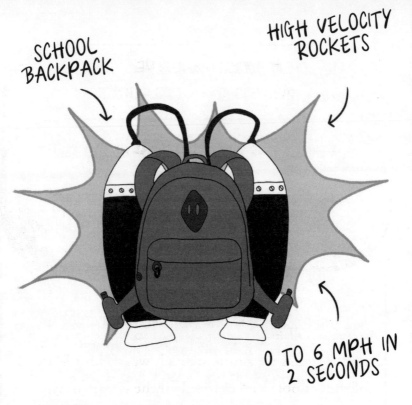

SCHOOL BACKPACK

HIGH VELOCITY ROCKETS

0 TO 6 MPH IN 2 SECONDS

The jetpack looked cool but with my luck, it was destined to be a recipe for **DISASTER**.

OK, OK, YOU GOT ME.

THAT WAS JUST A LITTLE JOKE.

TIP #2 (FOR REAL):

SNEAK ESCAPE.

BULLIES ARE AVOIDABLE IF YOU KNOW THE BEST
ESCAPE ROUTES.

THE CHEAT BOOK's pages began to turn again and stopped on a blueprint. It was a floor plan of the school. I recognised all the classrooms, lockers, hallways – everything!

Right by Ms Drood's class a line of ink *glowed*, illuminating a spidery path that snaked out of the classroom, down a corridor, around a corner and into the boys' toilets.

And then out of a window that led to a back fence with a hole in it, and through it, to my bus stop across the street.

I'd never been so **AMAZED** and **SPOOKED OUT** at the same time.

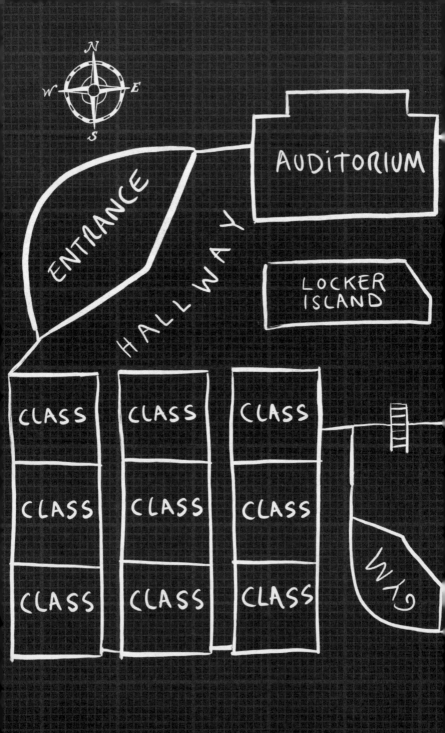

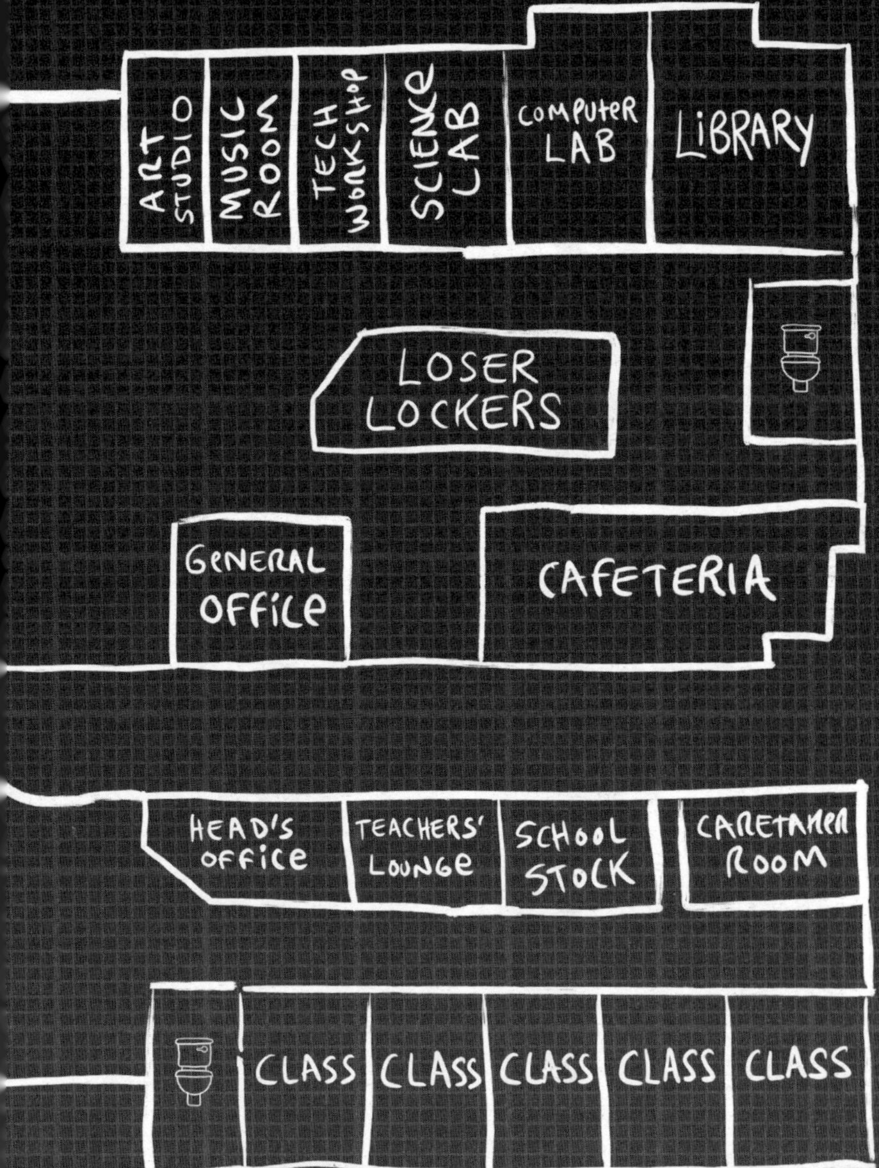

ART STUDIO

MUSIC ROOM

TECH WORKSHOP

SCIENCE LAB

COMPUTER LAB

LIBRARY

LOSER LOCKERS

GENERAL OFFICE

CAFETERIA

HEAD'S OFFICE

TEACHERS' LOUNGE

SCHOOL STOCK

CARETAKER ROOM

CLASS

CLASS

CLASS

CLASS

CLASS

Then, as if on cue, the end-of-school bell rang.

It was 'go time'!

Somehow, someway, the Ogre had found me out and caught up with me – he was **BLOCKING** the hole in the wire fence. The final exit in my escape.

'I knew you'd run,' he sneered. 'I know every way out of this poxy school and figured you'd pick this one because you're sneaky like that.'

I was in **BIG** trouble. The Ogre had a mad look in his eyes like he was going to rip my arms off and punch me with my own fists!

A crowd began to form behind the wire fence. They were all egging the Ogre on.

TRAITORS!

People say that at the point of death, your entire life flashes in front of your eyes, but instead all I could see was what *THE CHEAT BOOK* had told me to do next.

It was now or never. My dignity or my life.

I took a deep breath and then did what I had to do.

CLUCK!
CLUCK!
I'M A CHICKEN!

There was **STUNNED** silence at first. The wall of astonished school kids **SQUISHED** up against the wire fence were in complete shock at the scene **UNFOLDING** before their eyes.

And then they burst out laughing.

After a few stunned seconds, the Ogre snapped out of his confusion, gnashed his teeth and curled his meaty hands up into **CHUNKY** fists.

Everything seemed to go in slow motion.

The Ogre lunged slowly towards me like he was moving under water. I moved out of the way and watched him **STUMBLE** forward, off balance.

My backpack swung across my back and accidentally **WHACKED** him on his bum and he toppled over.

The monster had fallen! **AGAIN!**

But unlike Godzilla, the Ogre did not spring back into action. Instead, he just sat there on the ground looking puffy, pathetic and bewildered as he tried to catch his breath. To be honest, I was just as stunned as he was.

That was when everyone started **CHEERING**.

Right on time, the bus pulled up across the street. Before the Ogre could react, I squeezed through the hole in the wire fence, pushed past the cheering crowd and made it across just in time.

Any other day, I would've ridden the bus all the way home and celebrated my **LUCKY ESCAPE** from the Ogre with a packet of crisps and a couple of fun levels of splatting aliens, but this afternoon I had to go to Quran lessons at my local mosque.

Every Wednesday and Saturday I am stuck in class with a bunch of absolute goofballs.

There is **RIZWAN**, whose parents send him to Quran school to get a rest from his endless pranking, leaving us to suffer his plastic poos and burp-machine antics.

Behind him sits **MO-BOT** (aka Monotone Mohamed) whose voice is so mind-numbingly dull that every time the imam asks him to recite a verse, I wish that I was listening to a Spotify playlist of road drills instead.

IMRAN (aka SOCKS) sits way in the back because his sock pong is so fierce that the mosque goes into a stage 3 smog alert every time he takes off his shoes.

But **GOLDEN BOY YUSEF** is the **WORST**!

All the grown-ups think he's the most adorable kid ever because he's so small and can recite half the Quran from memory, but that's all a devious trick!

His saint act is just a cover for his spying shenanigans, where he tells the mosque kids to bring him sweets or he will squeal their secrets to the imam.

Quran school would be totally unbearable if it wasn't for **AHMED**. He is the only normal kid in class, besides me. When we're bored, we draw silly cartoons in class.

In the middle of class today, the imam gave me a note to give to the teacher in the girls' class, which **UPSET** Yusef.

'No fair! I always deliver the notes to the girls' class,' he moaned.

'Exactly. That's why I am changing it up,' replied the imam.

This infuriated Yusef but he couldn't do anything about it but **GRUMBLE** to himself. To annoy him even more, I made sure to give him a smug smirk as I passed his desk on my way out.

I love going to the girls' class. Not because I'm into them or anything (I only have eyes for Keisha) but a bunch of the girls at mosque are boy-crazy and go ga-ga over me as soon as I walk in, which drives my sisters **MAD**.

'Ugh, what are you doing here?' Samira asked, rolling her eyes.

Their teacher was nowhere to be seen so I placed the note on her desk.

'Oh my god, is that your brother? He is **SO** adorable!' One of the girls smiled. The Sister Beast sat in the corner, glaring at me as the other older girls all cooed and 'aww'ed.

'OK, I think you can go now,' the Sister Beast growled.

When I got back to the boys' side, I wondered if someone had **SNITCHED** to the imam about the fight I'd nearly had at school because, instead of his usual upbeat end of class messages, like:

> REMEMBER YOUR TRUE FAVE AND PRAY FIVE TIMES A DAY!

or

> DON'T BE GREEDY AND DROP MONIES FOR THE NEEDY

and

> MS MARVEL MOVIE DEBUTED AT NUMBER ONE! BISMILLAH!

That day, he ended with:

One of the most important characteristics of Islam is to protect people from harm. It is our duty to ensure that we treat people well and neither harm nor reciprocate harm.

I didn't mean to **HURT** the Ogre. It was all a strange and happy accident – but the imam's words still cut deep.

Maybe I should apologise. Well, that's if he doesn't **SQUASH** me first.

Turn on a fan, coz I'm heating up!

CHAPTER SEVEN

The next day at school, I walked through the corridor and the air was filled with a strange new atmosphere: **CALM** and **LAUGHTER**.

I checked my PopStock and saw that not only had my ranking gone **UP** by THREE but the Ogre's ranking had dropped to **ZERO**!

Gone was the manic panic of kids rushing to class before the Ogre stalked the halls; instead, kids were now pulling their locker doors all the way open without **FEAR** of being pushed inside them. I even saw a boy bend down to collect his can of cola from the vending machine, leaving himself wide open for a pantsing that never came.

We had entered a whole new world **WITHOUT** bullies.

A boy from the school's wrestling team came up to ask me what technique I had used to take down the Ogre, but I barely heard him because, at that moment, Keisha walked past.

'Hey, Kamal,' she said. *She knows my name!* 'I just wanted to say thanks for taking down the Ogre yesterday. He terrorised my little brother every day, you know. It's about time he got a taste of his own medicine.'

'It was, uh, my pleasure,' I said, my voice coming out all **HIGH-PITCHED**.

Keisha smiled and I watched her with heart-eyes as she walked away to her locker, not noticing that Wing and JoJo had arrived.

'Earth to Kamal,' said JoJo. 'If you stare any wider, your eyes will drop out.'

'Dude, I can't believe you smited the Ogre!' exclaimed Wing. 'How the heck did you manage that?'

'Oh, I might've had a little help.' I grinned, tapping my school bag knowingly.

'Well, I'm really disappointed in you, Kamal,' scolded JoJo. 'Fighting is so low IQ.'

'But it did wonders for his PopStock ranking,' Wing pointed out. 'You can sit with us now!' he continued, cheekily.

Even though he was joking, one look inside the cafeteria was all it took to see how quickly the rankings had **WIPED OUT** the old cliques and created new ones.

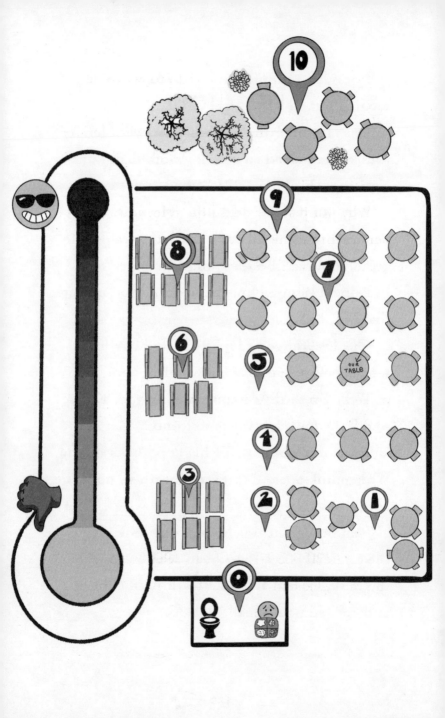

'I wonder what I'd need to do to get to the top ...'

'Well, if you wanna score a ten on PopStock, you're gonna have to do a lot more than knock Neville on his bum,' said Wing.

'Why not just be yourself and let your **GREAT** personality shine through and let more people get to know you?' added JoJo.

'Sounds like a lot of work. No, thanks,' I said. 'Instead, I'm gonna fast-track my way to the top, *CHEAT BOOK* style.'

I took *THE CHEAT BOOK* out of my school bag, placed it on the table and asked it: 'Hey, CB, what's the quickest way to become the **COOLEST** kid in school?'

The book opened on the right page.

AMBITIOUS LITTLE SQUIRT, AREN'T YOU?
WELL, THERE IS NO SINGLE ROUTE TO COOLNESS ...
THERE ARE THREE.

ROUTE #1:

BECOME A SUPERSTAR ATHLETE.
ONE WAY TO BE THE HERO, OR ENVY OF ALL,
IS TO WIN A TROPHY BY RUNNING OR HITTING A BALL.
IF YOU DREAM TO JOIN THE TEAM, TURN TO PAGE 34.

ROUTE #2:

JOIN THE KOOL KIDZ.
IT DOESN'T MATTER IF YOUR EARS ARE BIG
OR YOU HAVE A RED NOSE,
YOU CAN STILL LOOK COOL IF YOU WEAR
THE RIGHT CLOTHES.
IF YOU DECIDE TO GET BEAUTIFIED,
TURN TO PAGE 22.

ROUTE #3:

PLAY SOME TUNES.
IT DOESN'T MATTER WHAT STYLE YOU PLAY,
IF YOU DO IT WELL, YOU'LL SURELY SLAY.
IF YOU'RE WANTING TO GET THE PARTY JUMPING,
TURN TO PAGE 42.

'How does it **DO** that?!' cried Wing, poring over the book, looking for a socket.

'I'm more impressed by what it knows than what it does,' replied JoJo. 'It's like a gamebook where you get to decide what the characters do. Only the character in this book is actually you!'

'But aren't we all the main characters of our own stories?' asked Kamal.

'Yeah, except most of us don't have a book giving us the **SHORTCUTS**,' said Wing, pointedly.

'So, which route are you going to check out?' asked JoJo.

CHAPTER EIGHT

I bet you are all dying to know what I picked.

I chose the route that required **ZERO** money or good looks to enter, just a raw determination and an iron will: sports.

OPERATION ATHLETIC SUPERSTAR is GO!

The only problem was that all the team sign-ups were full except one: football team mascot.

At first, I refused. There was **NO WAY** I was jumping around in a dorky seal suit! But then Wing showed me that the kid who used to be the team mascot had a PopStock ranking of **EIGHT**.

At that moment, the wrinkly, pink bean inside my head that doctors call a brain had one of its rare bursts of sudden genius – a **GALAXY BRAIN** moment!

'If I was the team mascot and a player got injured, I'd have to play, right?'

'You're forgetting a couple of things,' said Wing. 'One, there'd have to be **ZERO OTHER SUBS**. And, two, you'd have to be able to play in the first place! News flash, Twinkle Toes – you can't kick a ball to save your life.'

But Wing's forgetting one thing too. I have *THE CHEAT BOOK.*

> DEFENDERS DON'T HAVE TO RUN OR HOLD THE BALL MUCH, CLEARING IT AWAY FROM THE GOAL IS THEIR MAIN JOB.

Defence it is, then. All I have to do is learn to pass a ball, which can't be **THAT** hard. I'll mostly be hanging back and letting the other players do all the legwork and then leech off their glory.

I love team sports!

'It's a textbook example of symbiosis,' said JoJo. 'Like the remora.'

'The remor-what?' said Wing and I at the same time.

'The remora is a fish that attaches itself to sharks with their big sucker mouths, **FEEDING** off their scraps,' answered JoJo. 'The largest ones are called "sharksuckers".'

'Am I the shark or the sucker?' I wondered out loud.

It didn't matter, because I was on the fast track to sports stardom. All I had to do was nab the unwanted spot as team mascot (**EASY**), and it would be a breeze from there.

Except, later that day, I walked past the sign-up sheet once more and I was no longer the only name!

What was *Humphrey* doing signing up for team mascot try-outs? On a **SECRET** mission for his dad, no doubt.

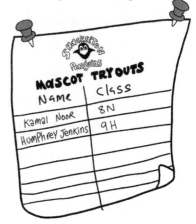

Fast forward to after school the next day.

I was standing in the back field with Humphrey and three other candidates. In our seal suits. Yesterday, I would've told you that team mascots were the **GOOFIEST** guys in sports, but a hundred cartwheels and tumble rolls later, I was convinced that it was harder to be a mascot than an Olympic gymnast.

As we were all catching our breath, Coach Stringer blew his whistle. 'Can anyone tell me what a team mascot is?' he asked.

Was that a trick question?

One kid always takes the bait, though. 'The person who wears a costume at the match?' they answered.

'GET OUT!' yelled Coach Stringer, and the kid ran off crying.

'No, a team mascot is the spirit of the team,' Coach Stringer explained, answering his own question. 'Its heart. When we're low, they pick us up, and when we're winning, they **CHEER** us on! Can you do it?'

At the end of try-outs, Humphrey and I were called into the coach's office.

I took a quick peek at *THE CHEAT BOOK*, which I'd smuggled into my **SMELLY** gym bag. And what it said completely took me by surprise.

YOU MUST be JOKing!

'You two were the best candidates,' Coach Stringer said. 'But I'm afraid we only have space for one mascot.'

If I lost to Humphrey, I'd have to switch schools.

'Humphrey, I'm afraid you are **NOT** our new mascot. Congratulations, Kamal!'

OMG! *THE CHEAT BOOK* was right! It had predicted this!

IMPRESSED, THE COACH WILL OFFER YOU A PLACE ON THE TEAM ...

Only with an **UNEXPECTED** twist.

AND YOU WILL HAVE TO POLITELY TURN HIM DOWN.

This was the opposite of what I wanted to do but *THE CHEAT BOOK* hadn't failed me yet. I just had to trust it.

'Thanks, Coach, but I can't accept,' I said, through gritted teeth. 'I think Humphrey would be a better mascot than me.'

'**REALLY?!**' replied Coach Stringer and Humphrey at the same time.

'Really,' I confirmed, pained.

'OK, Kamal. I respect your decision,' said Coach Stringer, shaking my hand. He then shook Humphrey's hand and congratulated him.

'Thank you, Coach,' Humphrey beamed. 'I can't wait to tell Dad!'

I'd never seen Humphrey quite so happy. Except maybe that one time he **RATTED** out the entire sixth form for turning the school swimming pool water into green jelly.

As Humphrey and I were heading out of the coach's office, Coach Springer called me back.

THEN SAY 'YES' TO WHATEVER YOU'RE OFFERED.

'I just remembered, there's one unadvertised position that a smart and **HONEST** lad like yourself would be perfect for.'

'There is?' I replied, pretending to be shocked.

A week later, at the Shackleton Penguins first game of the football season, Humphrey Jenkins made his debut as the new team mascot, and I, to Humphrey's total shock, sat in the dugout next to Coach Stringer as his new assistant team **MANAGER**.

This wasn't as cool as it sounded. I was basically the coach's dogsbody, carrying and fetching things. But it was the perfect place from which to **EXECUTE** my four-phase plan.

PHASE ONE

I trained with the team at practice for a couple of weeks, so I could get to know the players better and work on my passing.

I also watched a YouTube video on repeat called 'The Top 10 Best Passes Ever!' because, according to *THE CHEAT BOOK:*

> IT HAS BEEN PROVEN BY PRO COACHES THAT **WATCHING** A SPORT MAKES YOU **BETTER** AT THAT SPORT. IT'S CALLED 'VISUALISATION'.

PHASE TWO

The night before our big game against Thornbrook Rovers, I took a trip to the supermarket and bought a reduced carton of milk that was going off the next day because …

PHASE THREE

… on match day it was our pre-game ritual to have a cup of tea before the match, and the tea-making was my job.

I made sure that our three subs' tea got a **SPLASH** of last night's reduced milk.

> Poisoning your own teammates!? HAVE YOU NO SHAME!?

Don't be so melodramatic! A sip of spoiled milk isn't going to kill you. The worst you'll get is a little vomiting, stomach pain and …

PHASE FOUR

…EXPLOSIVE DIARRHOEA! MWAH HA HA!

The subs didn't make it out of the locker room toilets.

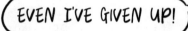

EVEN I'VE GIVEN UP!

The game was almost over and we were down 3–2 with Thornbrook all over us like ants on jam.

'LET'S GO, TEAM!' Coach Stringer sounded super confident but the sweat pouring down his face told a different story.

'WHO'S GOT THE SPIRIT? **I'VE GOT THE SPIRIT!** And that was Humphrey, our team mascot, cheering for himself.

Kevin, our midfielder, took the throw-in. Eyeing our winger, Corey, he tossed the ball over to him. Corey leapt up towards it, but so did the Thornbrook midfielder marking him.

We all knew what was coming.

CRUNCH!

The two boys' heads collided and they were both laid out on the ground, dazed.

'It's 3–3 and all our subs have the trots,' despaired Coach Stringer.

My devious scheme was no longer a dream – but **EVERYTHING** was on my shoulders now. As I ran on to the pitch I took a deep breath and remembered what I had to do.

> TO FAKE IT IN DEFENCE, RUN AROUND FREELY
> BUT ALWAYS KEEP ON THE EDGE OF THE ACTION.

I was all over the pitch, running like a blind dog in a meat market, trying to be everywhere but near the ball.

Not expecting the ball would come to me. **'WATCH OUT!'**

Looking up, the sun in my eyes, I couldn't see a thing and panicking, I kicked out. **BOOF!**

The ball swirled in a blustery wind. The crowd and the players all raised their heads, following its direction.

Soaring over their midfield, the ball landed – **PLONK!** – perfectly placed, in the open space between the Thornbrook defence and their goalkeeper.

Completely unmarked, our striker, Folarin, nimbly eased past Thornbrook's defence, his braids **FLAPPING** in the air as he chased my accidental assist.

Excitement shot through the crowd as Thornbrook's goalie came out to try to claim the ball. He **DIVED** towards it, but not close enough, as the ball sat just millimetres away from his outstretched fingertips.

Before he could react, Folarin dashed in and, with no one in his way, casually side-footed the ball into the corner of the net.

GOAL!

My teammates raced over and hoisted me up, bouncing me on their shoulders.

I'VE DONE IT! I'M A **SPORTS** STAR! This is what being a 10 must feel like.

The cheers grew louder as my teammates led the crowd in a chant:

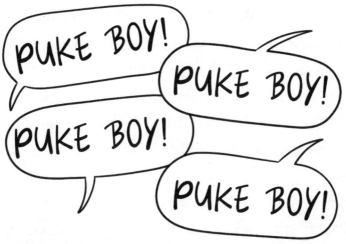

My blood ran cold. I'd just set up a match-winning goal (even if it *was* by accident) and they were **STILL** calling me Puke Boy?!

Later, Coach Stringer explained that insulting nicknames were what football was all about.

That it means that people like you.

'All the greats have it. Ever heard of "The Atomic Flea"?'

If I wanted to be part of the team, a mean nickname was something that I had to take on the chin. But that defeated the **ENTIRE** reason I had joined the football team in the first place.

There was only one way to handle this.

'You're **QUITTING** the team?!' said Coach Stringer, confused. 'But you're our star player.'

'I'm sorry, Coach,' I lied. 'But my parents want me to focus on school, not sports.'

'Alright, lad,' said Coach Stringer. 'School must take priority but the door will be open when your grades get better.'

'So, you have an assistant manager vacancy?' grinned Humphrey, poking his head through the door.

'Not for **EAVESDROPPERS**!' yelled Coach Stringer.

Leaving his office, I checked my popularity rankings and I had only moved up **ONE** place!

There must have been a mistake. I deleted the

PopStock app, downloaded it again but saw that I was still only a lousy 5!

'Hey, *CHEAT BOOK*. I'm a football sensation, so why have I only moved up one place in the popularity rankings?'

ISN'T IT OBVIOUS? YOU WILL SLOW DOWN YOUR RISE, IF YOU'RE NOT CHOOSY ABOUT WITH WHOM YOU FRATERNISE.

What did that even mean?

DUMP YOUR LOSER FRIENDS!
CUT THEM LOOSE OR WATCH YOUR RANK TANK.

THE CHEAT BOOK's advice was harsh but true. After all, how would I get to the cool table if I was still sitting with the 6s or 7s?

You can't get to the top of the cool chain without making some sacrifices.

'Like your sanity?' said Wing, when I told him and JoJo what *THE CHEAT BOOK* instructed at

143

break. 'Because you're talking **NONSENSE** right now.'

'Y'know, Wing, I think you're on to something,' said JoJo.

'I am?' asked Wing, shocked.

JoJo agreeing with Wing? I took a peek out of the window for flying pigs.

'I have a theory that there's a tiny part of the human brain that is devoted to being cool,' explained JoJo. 'And in Kamal, this part has **SWOLLEN** way up and squished all the other parts like **COCKROACHES**, and now, cool is all he thinks about.'

'Not true!' I argued. 'I think about lots of other stuff, actually.'

'You do?' asked JoJo, sceptically. 'Name one.'

JoJo and Wing both crossed their arms at the same time and glared at me.

I tried to think of other stuff I thought about, I really did, but all I could picture in my mind was sitting at the cool table.

'OK, maybe you're right,' I admitted. 'But this is just temporary. Think of it as a friendship time out.'

'That's not how friendship works,' said JoJo. 'You can't just **DUMP** us and then pick us back up when it's convenient, like we're dolls. You're either our friend or you're not. Which is it?'

Wing and JoJo both glared at me again, waiting for my answer.

'Then, I guess … I'm not,' I said.

Wing frowned. JoJo looked at the floor. I swallowed hard. What was this **FEELING**?

Pity? Regret? *Shame?*

Before I guilt-tripped myself into taking it back, the bell rang and I scurried off to my next class.

OMG! I'm so close to cool I'm practically chilly!

CHAPTER NINE

This was **WILD!**

Over just one maths class, my ranking had somehow shot up **THREE PLACES**!

I was now as cool as the school's hottest athletes and only two places away from being top of the cool chain.

But how? I did nothing to earn this. In fact, I did everything to **RUIN** my cool cred. I quit the football team and ditched the only two friends that I had, making me a Puke Boy with no actual mates.

Yet, somehow, I was getting *cooler*?

To make matters weird, a crowd had gathered in front of my locker. When I pushed through them and saw the note taped to my locker, suddenly **EVERYTHING** made sense.

GREETINGS!
You have been
cordially invited for
lunch at the quad.
Signed, the IOs.

WOW! THIS WAS MAJOR!

Every kid in Shackleton Academy would
give their right arm to have lunch with the
IOs! An invite was just one step away from
being a member. It meant Power! Prestige! It
was the best thing that could happen to a kid,

I could arrange that.

other than gaining uncanny
SUPERPOWERS in a freak
accident.

The note explained my
sudden epic cool bump but it
didn't explain why I got the
invite in the first place. It was
all too good to be true, but I
wasn't gonna look a gift horse
in the mouth.

By the time lunch rolled around, I was a
TREMBLING mess.

The quad is what we call the bandstand in the
back field where the 10s hang out. For the first
time ever, I wasn't eating at the cafeteria with
the normie **NOBODIES** – I had a seat at the table
of the Gods.

I was so nervous that I focused on my 'cool
dude' strut a little too much, and I almost
walked past the quad, but a familiar voice cried
out behind me: 'Kamal!'

149

It was Keisha. 'Come sit with us.'

'**YES!** I mean, sure, whatever,' I shrugged, remembering to play it cool last second.

Keisha was obvs a 10 and she introduced me to her double-digit buddies who were all **DEAD** impressed about the goal I helped score

yesterday and how I was the only kid to have had a run-in with Neville the Ogre who still had their head attached to their body.

'Generally, I try to have fun and not get on anyone's bad side,' I said. 'But it's impossible to stay off the Ogre's bad side coz it's the only side he's got!'

Everyone laughed except one boy, Patrick, who seemed really annoyed that Keisha was laughing at my joke. I didn't care, though, because I was **BUZZING**!

I was **FINALLY** on the cool table and I was making everyone laugh. Which felt good.

At first.

patrick

150

Then I realised that popular kids always laugh. Even when **NOTHING'S** funny.

'I always wondered what sitting at this table would be like. Awesome view and nice fresh-cut grass smell. It's a little far from everyone else, though.'

'Pfft, of course. Who'd want to be near those dorks?' said Patrick. 'Just look at them.'

A **WHIZZING** noise cut through the air and we all looked over to see Wing and JoJo on the back field, playing Fricket.

Seeing them playing together made me wish I was out there **GOOFING** around with them.

Just as I was starting to second-guess myself, Keisha came and sat next to me. 'Kamal, I'm having a **PARTY** this weekend. Can you come?'

I popped my collar and with half-closed eyes, said, 'I can try to stop by,' which was cool-kid talk for 'I'm in,' and Kamal talk for, 'KEISHA JUST INVITED ME TO A PARTY!?'

Keisha's invite was not only **SPONTANEOUS** but paperless, arriving with a PING notification on my phone.

This is not just any party but it's my first **BIG KID** party!

Y'know, the type where there's dancing and no magicians.

Is it even a party without a rabbit popping out of a hat?

Great! I get a lie-in.

I know if I'm not careful I might say or do something **STUPID** that'll plunge my cool rating into the social abyss.

THE CHEAT BOOK has a lot of clever party hacks, but it can't help me with my biggest problem: getting Keisha to like me!

Fortunately, I know exactly who to go to for advice.

Unfortunately, it's 1/3 of the **SISTER BEAST**.

Yasmin has over 4,000 chumps following her fashion tips online, so she **MUST** know something about impressing people.

I'm too smart to dabble with matters of the heart!

Actually, I have over 4,002 followers now!

I suspected Yasmin wasn't going to help me for **FREE** – and I was right.

YASMIN'S LIST OF DEMANDS

MAKE HER SANDWICHES
WHENEVER SHE'S HUNGRY

GIVE HER MY SCREEN TIME
FOR A WEEK

BE HER UNPAID PHOTOGRAPHER

GIVE PEDICURES ON DEMAND

'Alright, **RECRUIT**,' said Yasmin, 'boot camp begins exactly sixty minutes from now. The three areas we will cover are conversation, attitude and dancing.'

And exactly one hour later, Yasmin and I were at the food court in the shopping mall. She brought her friend Zahra to be my conversation partner because it would be 'proper **ICK**' if I ran lines on her.

'OK, remember what we discussed on the walk over here?' asked Yasmin. 'The three **GOLDEN** rules of conversation?'

'Uh, ask the girl about herself, **DON'T**
interrupt and APA,' I answered.

'Which stands for?'

'Always Pay Attention.' Easy.

'Good. Now let's see what you've got,'
said Yasmin.

I don't think I've ever had a
conversation with a girl that wasn't 'Pass
the ketchup' or 'Can I have a peek at your
science homework, JoJo?' but how **HARD**
could it possibly be? It was just talking.

Zahra smiled politely, waiting for me to
speak.

'H-how are, uh, do-o you hav—oh! You
have shoes! I have shoes on too! These are
my everyday trainers but I have ones for
skateboarding and ninja plimsoles for late-
night raids in the kitchen—'

*YASMIN PARTY-TRAINING SCORE CARD:
CONVERSATION SCORE: FAIL!
DON'T MONOLOGUE!

The next afternoon, Yasmin summoned me for an **ATTITUDE** lesson before Quran school.

'Rather than explain attitude to you, I thought I'd just show you,' said Yasmin. 'Behold! The finest hunk of all time: Timotei Shalabae!'

I was then subjected to a slideshow of magazine covers and movie clips where I had to study his 'runway **SWAGGER**'.

Smiling was out; instead, I had to master an expression that looked like I had just **FARTED**.

ATTITUDE SCORE: PASS!
YOU HAVE MEDIOCRE SWAGGER BUT ABOVE-AVERAGE CHEEKBONES THANKS TO SHARING **DNA** WITH ME.

For the dancing portion of my party training, Yasmin strong-armed me into wearing one of her old leotards. Thankfully our class wasn't in ballet club but our living room, safe from **JUDGING** eyes.

157

'Dance class 101: the foxtrot,' said Yasmin.

'How about a dance from **THIS** century?' I asked.

'What, no love for the classics? OK, let me show you how it's done,' said Yasmin.

She **LAUNCHED** herself into the air with a scissor kick and, once her feet were on the floor again, she started **FLAPPING** her hands and **HOPPING** from one foot to the other with an intense look on her face.

She then dropped to the floor and started **ROLLING** and **WIGGLING**.

'Yasmin, I have a question.'

'Shoot,' she said, out of breath.

'Have you ever actually been to a big kid party?'

'Um, no,' confessed Yasmin. 'Well, I threw a rave on The Sims once. I earned seventy party points. Thank you, username **hanging_ with_my_gnomies**.'

What a scam!

I couldn't believe I'd given her my screen-time for a week and agreed to be her pedicure slave.

But there's no time to be mad because Keisha's party is tonight and I am even more **CLUELESS** now about girls than I was yesterday.

Fourteen panicked outfit changes later - it was **PARTY TIME**!

When I arrived at Keisha's house, I couldn't hear any music. Maybe the DJ was late? Anyway, I gave my hair a quick ruffle, popped the millionth mint into my blisteringly fresh mouth and pressed the doorbell.

Keisha's dad opened the door and led me down to the party in the basement.

When I walked in, I could not believe what I saw.

It was the kind of party where the tick of the clock was **LOUDER** than the music (Brahms, in case you were wondering).

Keisha's mum is a nutritionist, so all the party food was **'GOOD'** for us. There was juice instead of soda. Celery sticks instead of Kit Kats. Taramasalata?

Bleugh! Posh **PRISON** food!

Luckily, Mum had made me bring my own food to the party because we weren't sure whether there'd be Halal options.

Mum really put together a **SCRUMPTIOUS**
spread. So scrumptious, in fact, that I could feel
everyone's hungry eyes on me as I set it out on
the table.

'Anyone want to try some halwa?' I asked.

Everyone nodded, vigorously.

In a flash, they had all devoured my halwa,
GUZZLED down most of my orange soda and left
me with a half-eaten cheese toastie and a single,
shrivelled crisp.

This wasn't even the worst bit.

The rush of sugar and E numbers from my
food stirred everybody up until they **ERUPTED**
with a burst of frenzied energy, terrifying to
behold.

It was total **SUGAR** overload!

I don't think any of these kids had ever had a calorie that wasn't counted for them. But tonight, they were **UNCHAINED**!

Keisha's parents were furious, of course. But despite the **MASSIVE** clean-up afterwards and the telling-off they all got from their parents on the way home, this made me a hit!

So much so, that at school on Monday, the 10s voted to keep me as a permanent member, making me a **10**!

WOOHOO! MISSION ACHIEVED!

But remember Patrick? That cool kid I told you about earlier who didn't seem very happy that Keisha was so nice to me? Well, *he* was steam-out-of-the-ears **FURIOUS** that everyone liked me so much.

So, he challenged me to a 'Cool-Off'.

A 'Cool-Off' is a duel of the cool where the loser is **BANISHED** from the clique. Once a challenge is made you **HAVE** to accept.

After I got a briefing on the rules, Patrick and I were led to the back field to begin our **SHOWDOWN**.

And here they go!

Patrick makes the first move. Unleashing a perfect 'whatever' shrug.

But Kamal counters with a CLASSIC 'who cares?' Eye roll.

Patrick hits back with a SKILFUL twirl and placement of a DEVASTATINGLY COOL pair of shades.

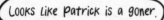

But Kamal retaliates, flaunting a vintage guitar badge and pressing it, unleashing an epic GUITAR SOLO!

ROCK ON!

Looks like Patrick is a goner.

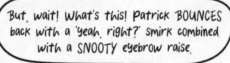

But, wait! What's this! Patrick BOUNCES back with a 'yeah, right?' smirk combined with a SNOOTY eyebrow raise.

Kamal stumbles. He's on the ropes!

Patrick takes it home with a PUNISHING 'what a loser' tut and head shake.

And it's ALL OVER for Kamal!

RIP
KAMAL'S COOLNESS

Being a good sport, I congratulated Patrick, who said, 'The **BEST** man always wins – ME! HA! HA! HA!'

What a **SMUG** idiot!

This is nothing but a small setback and I *will* find another way to the top, just you wait!

CHAPTER TEN

The next day I was back at the school activity board to see if there were any extracurriculars that I could be extra-spectacular in.

The Shackleton Academy talent show was anything but. There was **ZERO** talent and it was more of a catastrophe than a show.

Every year we were forced to sit through a snore-fest of awful acts, because every year it was the same **BORING** kids doing the same boring routine.

But what if there was an act that was so exciting, so dynamic that it jolted the audience awake from their bore-comas with its sheer awesomeness?

It could be enough to **ROCKET** my rating from a six to a ten!

YES! I'm gonna transform this carnival of cringe into THE **GREATEST SHOW** ON EARTH!

But how? I don't have any talent except maybe mucking things up.

AW! DON'T BE SO DOWNHEARTED, PUT ON A SMILE AND GET THE PARTY STARTED!

I fixed *THE CHEAT BOOK* with my best **WITHERING** stare. 'I don't know if you've been paying attention but I pretty much destroyed the last party I was at, so.'

> WELL, THIS TIME ALL YOU HAVE TO DO IS PLAY SOME BANGING TUNES.

I couldn't learn an instrument in a **WEEK**!

> WHO SAID ANYTHING ABOUT LEARNING TO PLAY AN INSTRUMENT?
> I'M THE **CHEAT** BOOK NOT THE TEACH BOOK.
> I WILL SHOW YOU HOW TO COOK UP
> A **MONSTER BEAT**
> USING ONLY **TRICKS** AND **DECEIT**.

I will need a laptop.

At home we only have a family tablet that I share with my sisters. It can barely handle streaming their K-dramas, let alone help me produce a talent-show banger.

Wing and JoJo have laptops but we aren't friends any more. *Wait!* Ahmed will have a laptop. In fact, he'll have loads! His dad runs an electronics repairs and spares shop.

All I have to do is ask him at mosque later, if I can borrow one of his laptops.

During geography **(GROAN)**, I start brainstorming some DJ name ideas.

They were all **RUBBISH**!

As I went back to the drawing board, Mr Cornish was droning on about how well foxes have adapted to the city.

The foxes round my way raid our bins every week – just last night one of them wailed so loud I had to drag myself out of bed and yell out my window: **'SHUT IT, YOU CRAZY FOX!'**

AH! That's it!

With the abundant array of **EPIC** chin curtains, you would be forgiven for thinking that I had wandered into a beard convention, but actually I was at the mosque with my dad for Friday prayers.

I couldn't find Ahmed anywhere but I did spy golden boy Yusef. **UGH!**

There was no way I was praying next to that annoying show-off, so I tried to steer Dad away to the other side of the prayer hall – but it was too late. Yusef had spotted me and **WAVED** me over.

'Kamal, isn't that your friend from Quran school?' asked Dad.

'Yeah,' I sighed, defeated.

I trudged after Dad as he walked over to where Yusef and his dad were sitting, and we spread our prayer mats out next to them.

Friday prayers are always **PACKED** and today we were all crammed in tighter than a can of sardines. It was so bad that every time the imam cried 'Allahu Akbar!' and everyone went down on the floor into *sujood*, my head kept hitting the butt of the old man in front of me. It was **SO** embarrassing.

Yusef found this absolutely **HILARIOUS** and broke out into his high-pitched giggles every time it happened, but the joke was on him because when prayers were over, Yusef's dad made him pray again to make up for the prayers that he **RUINED** by laughing at me.

I ran into Ahmed outside mosque and he agreed to loan me an old laptop for a Charizard shiny card.

Forty-eight hours and a **BUNCH** of YouTube tutorials later, I had cooked up a dance banger worthy of my cool DJ name. But I still felt like I was missing something.

YOU NEED AN OUTFIT.
SOMETHING SHOW-STOPPING!

OH! I know! What if I wore a cool mask?

My crafting skills were rubbish, but Rizwan from Quran school is a wiz at building things. He was totally excited to come over to my flat to make a mask for me. Perhaps **TOO** excited.

Turns out he has a big **CRUSH** on Halima, my weird goth sister, and saw helping me as his opportunity to get in her good books. How devious. And **GROSS**.

When he was done, Rizwan's papier mâché creation was tricked out with more gadgets than Batman's utility belt.

I had this talent show in the bag!

⏩ **FAST FORWARD TO THURSDAY NIGHT!** ⏩

The school auditorium was **PACKED** for the talent show.

The lights went down and it was **GO TIME**!

First up was Maurice the Juggler (SNOOZE!), who was followed by Wing and JoJo, who put on the dorkiest magic show (CRINGE!), and then a breakdancing trio called 'The Supernovas' (more like 'super no').

Now it's my turn. **GULP!**

'What's up, Shackleton!' I yelled, taking to the stage.

AWKWARD SILENCE.

Tough crowd. I powered up the laptop and dropped the beat.

BOOM-BOOM-POW!

BOOM-BOOM-POW!

What came next was like something out of a **DREAM**. Everyone got up on their feet and started dancing to the beats I had created.

Even the Head was bobbing along from the side of the stage.

I was **CRUSHING IT**! For the first time ever at a school talent show, people were having fun.

My PopStock rating was going to be **STRATOSPHERIC**!

Everybody started cheering: KRAZY FOX! KRAZY FOX! KRAZY FOX!

WOOHOO! Sounds like 'Puke Boy' is officially dead!

Goodbye to the grossest nickname in school history and long reign Krazy Fox.

I could see it already: everyone fighting to have me DJ at all the birthday parties and I couldn't walk two steps without seeing someone rocking a Krazy Fox t-shirt. I'm gonna be a **LEGEND**!

Then suddenly my laptop screen went blue.

WUB-WUB-WUUUUUUUUUUUUUUUUUUB!

My bouncy beat glitched into a deafening drone that **BLEW UP** the auditorium speakers, shooting out sparks!

Kids screamed and teachers grabbed the fire extinguishers, spraying the speakers in foam.

Life moves pretty fast. One second you can have a whole crowd dancing to your beats and, a second later, you're left standing on a pile of **BROKEN** talent-show dreams.

SUB ZERO

My rating's so low, it's crashed thru the Earth's crust and is floating in space!

POPSTOCK RATING

CHAPTER ELEVEN

The next day, I was washing my hands in the boys' loos – and that's when I noticed it.

My reflection in the mirror in front of me started to **FADE** and I could see through my body to the stalls behind me.

Odd.

And then the dinner lady didn't seem to see me when I made my order. I **DROPPED** my coin on the counter to make a noise, but she just looked at me, but kind of *through* me at first, like I was only just coming into focus.

Then, later, in class, Ritesh sat on me like my seat was empty then **SPRANG** up and gave me the meanest look, as if I pulled a prank on him, when I was sitting there the whole time and he just didn't see me.

What was happening?

I had become one of those things that people saw but did not pay attention to, like recycling bins, or the 'No selfies in class' sign, or (shudder) teachers!

I was starting to think that being called 'Puke Boy' wasn't so bad after all. At least people acknowledged my existence. Now, they didn't see me **AT ALL**. I was a nobody. A pariah. A **GHOST** floating through the halls, aimless and hopeless.

That was it! I was done with school. I wanted out. Who needed boring teachers, mean kids, uncomfortable chairs and icky lunches? I was going to learn online and hang out with my virtual friends and build **SPECTACULAR** fortresses and take down alien armadas.

But convincing my parents to take me out of school was going to be more than a *Mission: Impossible*. It was going to be a *Mission: Out of the Question*.

But I'm not one to back down from a challenge. I just have to convince one person.

Luckily, Dad was in a good mood because for dinner, Mum made his favourite meal, *malai kismayo*.

SNIFF SNIFF

Mmmm! MaLai KismaYo smeLLs tasty. What is it?

It's fried fish, salad and flatbread. Stop drooling. We can't taste. We're imaginary, remember.

I waited until Dad had his first **BLISSFUL** bite before I put my **DEVIOUS** plan into action.

'So, uh, Dad,' I said. 'I read a really interesting article in the *Muslim Times*.'

'Oh, yeah?' said Dad, putting some fish on his flatbread with his fingers.

'Modern schools are a hive of crime and sin, Dad. It said, home schooling kids, especially boys, will make them more pious.'

I knew all the right buttons to push to scare Dad into giving me what I wanted. **MWAH HA HA!**

'Is this about the cool thing?' said Dad, narrowing his eyes.

WHAT THE CRUMBS!

How did he know? That sent me on a **PARANOIA** SPIRAL!

1) **IS he Psychic?**

2) **Has he bugged ALL my belongings?**

3) **DID JoJo + Wing TELL HIM BEHIND my BACK?**

Maybe it was a **LUCKY** guess? OK. Play it cool.

'What cool thing?' I replied, as cool as a cucumber drinking Slurpee on an Arctic beach.

'Yasmin tell me you be trying to be Mister Cool,' chuckled Dad, in English.

English coming out of my dad's mouth sounds a little off, like shoes that don't quite fit, but he **LOVES** to slip into it sometimes when he's trying to be funny.

But that isn't the important part – Yasmin had squealed on me!

BETRAYED by my own sister! I thought that kind of thing only happened in soap operas.

'What's wrong, son?' asked Dad, switching back to Somali. 'Your mother told me that you've been **SULKING** in your room all week.'

'It's my own *personal* problem. I'll get over it,' I

said, pushing my finished plate away. 'Gotta get some sleep. I have a busy day tomorrow of being invisible.'

'Well, you're not going to bed without a bit of Dad Wisdom.' A Dad Lecture, more like.

'I'm good, thanks.'

But as I got up off my chair to leave, Dad gave me one of his terrifyingly **STERN** glares, which made me sit right back down.

Then his stony face brightened and he said, 'Now, do you want "wise and kind" Dad, or "life is hard" Dad?'

'Can I get a combo? Kind but hard?' I replied.

'Sure,' said Dad. 'Kamal, you can be the king of England or heavyweight **CHAMPION** of the world, but no matter what you do, not everyone's going to like you. In fact, I bet you if you took a poll, you'd find that there are probably **LOTS** of people who don't like you.'

'Ouch! Easy on the "hard", Dad! Where's the "kind" part?'

'I like you,' said Dad, with a smirk.

'But you're my dad. You're supposed to like me. I bet even Thanos's dad liked him.'

'Yes, I love you because you are my child and also my test from Allah,' replied Dad. 'And you are *very* challenging.'

Mum let out a big chuckle as she loaded the dishwasher. Hey! I thought this was a lecture, not a **ROAST**!

'You have taught me patience but also gratitude, which I pass on to you,' continued Dad. 'You forget that we are blessed, Mashallah. There are people like us who are on boats stranded at sea. Languishing in camps. All dreaming of what we have. Be **THANKFUL**, Kamal.'

What do I say to that?

Mum and Dad always

pull out the 'BE GRATEFUL' card whenever they think we're acting spoiled or want us to eat our greens, but being grateful isn't going to **MAGICALLY** make me feel not left out or make my greens taste any less gross.

I really feel bad for refugees who haven't been as lucky as my family and are still struggling to find a safe place to live, but I also want to warn them that their troubles won't totally end if they make it over here.

I always do

Some people will be really mean to them; they'll feel homesick and miss all the people they lost in the chaos; they're going to hate the weather (it's **SO COLD** and **RAINY**); and, most importantly, school sucks.

But I guess it is better than living in danger every single day.

So, Dad won.

I'll keep going to school, but I'm not going to **PRETEND** to like it.

CHAPTER TWELVE

I was getting used to life as a nonentity.

Even *THE CHEAT BOOK* seemed to be out of ideas.

But there were some pluses to being a social ghost.

I could walk through Bullies Boulevard **UNPOUNDED**.

I could sneak an **EXTRA** muffin at lunch.

And I could come to school dressed up as a **CLOWN** and nobody would blink an eye.

At assembly, the Head announced that the nominations for school captain would be coming up.

School captains are basically team mascots but for the entire school. They have to go to a lot of school meetings and events and help organise assemblies. Sounds like a lot of extra work for a crummy badge. No thanks.

Then I had **ANOTHER** galaxy brain moment. School captains also get to decide the lunch menu, boss the prefects around and even get a discount at the school tuck shop.

With these privileges I could do **FAVOURS** for people who would then all owe me and, in no time, I'd have everyone wrapped around my little finger.

Who needs to be cool when you have **POWER**! **MWAH HAHAHA!**

But I would have competition. On the school notice board there were two candidates on the school captain nominee sign-up sheet: Humphrey Jenkins – and Reepicreep, the school rat.

'A **RAT**? Doesn't anyone take this election seriously?' I wondered out loud.

'Why would they?'

I spun around to see Texas Jeff, the caretaker, kneeling down in the hallway in his usual cowboy hat and boots, mending a radiator. 'The school cap'n elections have always been a one-horse race, kid,' said Texas Jeff. 'Humphrey always wins.'

'Well, not this time, partner,' I said, adding my name to the sign-up sheet. 'Because a new bronco has joined the rodeo.'

The next day the candidates were announced over the school's PA system.

WHAT! JOJO SIGNED UP?!

The nominees for school captain are Humphrey Jenkins, Reepicreep the school rat, Kamal Noor and Jyoti Joshi.

187

This was bad. Humphrey had been school captain two years in a row. He was like an old pair of socks that **NEEDED** changing for new ones: me.

But JoJo wasn't just a fresh pair of socks, she was a whole new wardrobe. She was smarter than us, more talented and had the most heart.

Normally, I'd be sunk. But I had one thing that JoJo didn't have: *THE CHEAT BOOK.*

You can't win an election without a stance – a belief that'll inspire people to vote for you.

Humphrey's stance was, 'Everything is good, let's keep it that way.'

JoJo's stance was that 'School should and could be better' by being eco-friendly and providing free breakfasts for students.

I flipped open *THE CHEAT BOOK* for some inspiration.

YOUR OPPONENTS ARE BOTH SPEAKING ABOUT THE THINGS THAT ARE IMPORTANT TO THE STUDENTS THAT VOTED, BUT MOST STUDENTS COULDN'T BE BOTHERED TO VOTE AT ALL. YOU HAVE TO **AMAZE** THE **UNFAZED!**

So, I made my stance a simple one that all students could get behind: **FUN!**

I promised a waterslide in the school swimming pool and free robot dogs for every student.

Sure, these promises were **BONKERS** and I probably couldn't make them happen, but it was like *THE CHEAT BOOK* told me:

> ELECTION PLEDGES ARE ABOUT **EXCITEMENT**. WORRY ABOUT FULFILLING THEM AFTER YOU WIN.

Another election must is a **CATCHY** slogan. A short, memorable phrase that tells people what I'm about.

I reckoned that most students felt like I did and thought that secondary school was a nightmare and secretly wished that they were still in primary school with all its nap time, jungle gym and no wrong answers. So, my slogan was ...

You're not going to be able to talk to every student, so posters are an important tool for **WINNING** an election.

Being the principal's son, Humphrey had free access to the general office to help him print his posters, which were all pretty bland-tacular.

JoJo's art skills were just as poo as Humphrey's but she had the brains to hire Wing, whose creative genius crafted eyepopping posters that **WOWED** the whole school.

Touché, guys. But Kamal has now entered the chat.

I hit back with a two-hit promo combo. I put up posters between all the water fountains that said **'THIS DRINK IS ON ME – VOTE KAMAL'.**

I also put posters up made from silver mirror card that said **'LOOK WHO'S VOTING FOR KAMAL'** and placed them in strategic mirror spots in school: at the main entrance (first look of the day), on corners (perfect for avoiding prefects), and outside toilets (double check you're not trailing any toilet roll as you leave).

BUT POSTERS ARE NOT GOING TO BE ENOUGH. IF YOU REALLY WANT TO COME OUT ON TOP, YOU HAVE TO GO TO PLACES OTHERS CAN'T. THE HEART OF EFFECTIVE ELECTION ADVERTISING IS A GOOD SMEAR CAMPAIGN.

Give it a go, sounds like fun.

Don't listen to him, getting you in a fix is how he boosts his ticks!

Under the cover of a toilet break, I was let out in the middle of triple German, where I then ran through the corridors slapping cheeky stickers on my rivals' election posters.

Don't flush your vote.

You Guac 2B Kidding Me!

Of course, Humphrey and JoJo tried to point the finger at me, but they couldn't **PROVE** it.

It's not my fault that I have passionate supporters.

Now it was time to hit the streets and meet the peeps.

Humphrey was so sure that the kids who voted for him before would support him again, he held zero meet and greets.

JoJo made a passionate speech in the middle of the school cafeteria. Most people ignored her except the geeks who **LOVED** her idea of forming an Avengers team of our school's brightest minds to help turn it into a tech paradise.

I locked in the sports crew by promising them an extension if homework fell on the same day as a game. I reeled in the cool clique with my plan to have a party at the end of **EVERY** term. Music club fangirls were over the moon when I told them that I planned to bring more quirky instruments to school, and the gym bods were so pumped about my proposal to add body-building meal plans to the school lunch menu, they hoisted me into the air.

The campaign had flown by, and it was the day before voting. We had to make a speech to our whole year and then have a debate.

According to *THE CHEAT BOOK*, there was no point in entering a debate without having a batch of sassy comebacks ready to **UNLEASH** on your opponents.

REMEMBER YOU'RE ON STAGE, SO BE ENTERTAINING.

I had a short list of debate zingers written down that I taped to the inside of my locker door so I could memorise them between classes.

THE CHEAT BOOK's campaign was foolproof.

Or was it?

Meanwhile . . .

As Kamal got ready for his next class, he was unaware that he was being WATCHED

'Welcome to the school captain election debate,' announced our Science teacher, Mr Kandasamy. In a twinkling green-sequinned waistcoat, and with the long ends of his normally **DROOPING** moustache curled straight up, he looked just like a circus strongman.

Mr Kandasamy began the debate by reading out the predicted election poll results.

I was first, followed by JoJo. Humphrey was tied third with Reepicreep.

'Now, without further of ado, let's meet the candidates,' said Mr Kandasamy.

First to introduce themselves was Humphrey.

'My fellow Year Eights. You know me. I'm a Jenkins, and we were born to lead,' said Humphrey. 'Who saw you through the candy shortage of last year?'

Humphrey pointed the microphone at the crowd and the auditorium yelled,

YOU DID!

'Who took on and defeated Newdale in the Minecraft challenge without the loss of a single life?' said Humphrey, then pointed his microphone back at the crowd.

YOU DID!

'That's right, I did! So, be there for me tomorrow, so I can be there for you,' said Humphrey, to deafening applause.

Humphrey turned to JoJo and me. 'Follow that!' he hissed.

JoJo was up next.

'Fellow Shackletonians! I have a dream!' cried JoJo. 'Well, more of a vision, really. Imagine a school captain who shares their **POWER** with a league of students made up  from the brightest and boldest from every class. Imagine an eco-friendly school where waste is **ERASED**. So, vote for me, because a vote for JoJo is a vote for the future!'

A ripple of polite claps echoed around the
auditorium.

Now it was my turn.
**'WASSUP,
SHACKLETON!'** I yelled
into the microphone.
'Now, I know how bored
you guys must be, being
forced to sit through this
snooze-fest. Feels like
when your parents make you
sit down and watch the news,
amiright?'

The crowd cheered in agreement.

'Well, I promise that if you vote for me
tomorrow, I'll ban school captain debates!'

The audience **BURST** out cheering,
stamping their feet. Mr Kandasamy didn't look
impressed.

'Eat that!' I said to Humphrey.

Now, with the introductions out of the way,
the debate began.

'Humphrey,' asked Mr Kandasamy, 'please

tell us what you would do first as
school captain?'

'I will put the cost of
everything in the tuck shop
down to fifty pence!' said
Humphrey, to a lukewarm
reaction.

'Same question to you, Jyoti,' said Mr
Kandasamy.

'I will start a collection drive for all—' began
JoJo.

'BALDERDASH!' screamed Humphrey. 'Isn't
it true that you promised that the first thing
you'd do as school captain was to give anyone
who has a perfect A average, like you, a three-
day weekend, but make anyone with grades
below come to school on Saturdays?' smirked
Humphrey.

Gasps of outrage spread across the audience.

'No! That isn't what I said!' cried JoJo, but the
audience had already starting **BOOING** her.

'And what would you do on your first day,
Kamal?' asked Mr Kandasamy.

'I'd buy a pool table for the—'

'HOGSWASH!' screamed Humphrey again. 'Wasn't it your job as assistant football coach to make the team a cup of tea before the big game?' he asked.

'Yeah? So what?' I replied.

'Why did you make it with spoiled milk, unless you wanted to make the subs sick so you could go on and pull off a **FLUKEY** assist?!' cried Humphrey, whipping out the empty reduced milk carton and holding it up in the air.

How had he got it? I hid it in my locker but forgot to throw it out.

Turning dramatically to the audience, he asked them, 'How can you vote for someone who **POISONS** his own classmates?!'

What a **DWEEB**! It was time to unleash all the witty comebacks I'd been memorising.

Humphrey was in for it now.

Brace yourselves, readers, because you're about to hear talk so **TRASHY** that JoJo will want to sort it for recyclables.

'Oh, yeah?' I said. 'Well, you're ...'

The hot, blinding spotlight beaming down on the stage had fried my mental hard drive, because every time I searched my memory banks for a wicked burn all I got back was **'ACCESS DENIED'**.

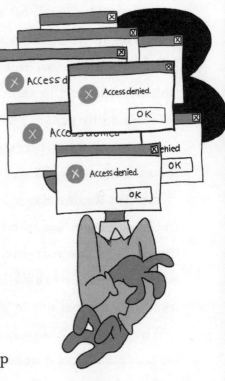

I just stood there, wishing the ground would open up and swallow me.

Somewhere in the jeering audience, Neville smiled, his mission complete.

Then, miraculously, something **BUBBLED** up to the surface from the depths of my brain like a Magic 8 Ball answer.

'Two years, he's been school captain,' I said, pointing to Humphrey, 'and Humphrey doesn't know any more about leadership than a turkey knows about Christmas.'

A smattering of laughter came from the audience. Humphrey looked around, anxiously.

'You may be the son of the Head,' I said, 'but the way you've been debating today, I think we should call you The Butt!'

The auditorium exploded with laughter. The Year Sevens were in stitches, tears streaming down their faces! The older kids **CLAPPED** and **WHISTLED** admiringly.

Humphrey couldn't believe how badly things had turned and marched off stage, furious.

Mr Kandasamy called off the debate early and everyone rushed out to place their votes.

The mystery of how Humphrey managed to get that reduced milk carton was solved when I got back to my locker and found the

door hanging off
its hinges, my
school bag open
and all my stuff
SCATTERED across
the floor.

All but one
thing that turned
out to be missing.
THE CHEAT BOOK!

CHAPTER THIRTEEN

While my locker was being fixed, I had to use a temporary locker that was so far away it might as well have been at the edge of the universe.

Luckily, I made it into form room just in time to hear the election results over the school PA system.

After yesterday's blistering debate, the votes are now in. The winner, in a landslide victory is ... KAMAL NOOR!

A deafening **CHEER ERUPTED** and I was instantly swamped with high-fives and back slaps. Even my form teacher Mr Norris got in on the action by shaking my hand and congratulating me on my big win.

The school captain inauguration will be this afternoon. Have a good day.

The bell rang for the start of lessons and my adoring crowd parted, revealing JoJo in a **BLUBBER OF TEARS** at her desk and Wing comforting her. I hadn't known how much being school captain would have meant to her.

206

I wanted to walk over and thank her for a good election race, but it felt a lot like **GLOATING**, so I went to my next lesson instead.

The second I stepped into the school corridor, all the talking stopped and like a **ZOMBIE MOVIE**, everyone stopped what they were doing and ran towards me with hungry eyes and big creepy smiles.

I tried to make a break for it but I was leapt on at all sides by crazed kids **CLAMOURING** for a piece of me.

Caught in an endless rotation of adoration, I was starting to feel like a sock in a tumble dryer, until I was rescued by two bigger boys in dark sunglasses, who pulled me out of the barrage of **GRASPING** hands and smartphone flashes.

'I'm Reggie,' said the ginger one, 'and the other one's Clive. We're your bodyguards.'

'Uh, OK?' I said.

Being school captain means I get two bodyguards but also an 'entourage' (that's French for 'suck-ups who follow you everywhere') and a personal assistant. Mine was a Year Seven boy called Jarvis whose job was to keep me updated with my new **BUSY** schedule.

'The school choir has written a piece for your inauguration and needs you to listen to it for approval,' said Jarvis. 'And the gym bods want you to open their new Aqua yoga pool.'

'Only if I get the first dip in it,' I joke.

'Oh, and one more thing,' said Jarvis. 'The Tens have invited you to join their ranks.'

I whipped out my phone, fired up the popularity app and my jaw **HIT** the floor.

OFF THE CHARTS

Trading favours with all the different school cliques during my campaign had **SKYROCKETED** me to the top spot.

I was now the coolest kid in school.

'Don't look so shocked, sir,' smiled Jarvis. 'You're a star.'

A STAR!

Fast forward and it was now time for the school captain inauguration. I was standing backstage, where just weeks ago I **PUKED** in front of the entire school and this whole bonkers quest to be cool started.

The Head was onstage giving a speech about the **IMPORTANCE** of voting and blah blah blah.

CLAP!
CLAP!
CLAP!

I spun around to see Humphrey glaring at me, hiding something behind his back.

'Congratulations, school captain,' he sneered. 'I thought *you* had outsmarted me, but it turns out that you had help.'

Humphrey revealed what he was hiding: *THE CHEAT BOOK.*

'THAT'S MINE!'

'Now **EVERYTHING** makes sense. How you became assistant football coach, how you won the school captain vote.'

'GIVE IT BACK!'

'Not yet.' Humphrey smirked. 'I want you to quit being school captain and give the job to me. It's mine and you **STOLE** it.'

'Or what?'

'Or I show this book to my dad and tell him how you **CHEATED** to get this job,' answered Humphrey. 'You'll probably be expelled, and then I'll feed this book into the shredder.'

'Why haven't you shown the Head already?' I asked.

'It's more fun this way,' said Humphrey. 'I want to see that **CRUSHED** expression on your face when you have to give your dream up.'

'You're horrid, Humphrey,' I said. 'I was going to change things. Make this school a fun place.'

'**CHANGE?**' Humphrey laughed. 'You think you can change things? School captain is a ceremonial role, dummy! They're not going to give real power to a twelve-year-old.'

'Then why do you want to be school captain so badly?' I asked.

'My dad was school captain for his whole time at school, and I will be too,' said Humphrey.

Before I could answer, the Head's **BOOMING** voice cried out on the microphone: 'Ladies and gentleman, let's welcome our new school captain ... **KAMAL NOOR**!'

'It's now or never,' Humphrey hissed.

I walked on to the stage.

I could feel that nauseous cauldron of tension start churning in my belly again.

The Head handed me the honorary school captain sash. When I put it

213

on, the auditorium exploded with applause.

'Go on, son,' said the Head, gesturing to the microphone in front of me.

I looked out into the cheering audience and thought back to the first time I had stood in front of them. I had been so **NERVOUS** and **ASHAMED** about them learning about who I really was that my nerves had got the better of me and I became Puke Boy, that freaky refugee kid who **VOMMED** all over the Head.

After that incident, I'd pinballed from **EPIC FAIL** to **CRINGE CATASTROPHE**, all in the hope that I would eventually become the right person to join the right group and everyone would think I was cool.

Now that I am cool, it's not as *cool* as I thought it would be.

Being cool is high maintenance. All it would take is one naff joke, the wrong sneakers, or a missed goal and I'd be **UNCOOL** again, and everyone would turn their backs on me.

But Wing and JoJo never did.

I spotted them in the audience, and they were

cheering and clapping for me even though I had ditched them to **'BE COOL'**. Which I could see now was the most uncool thing I have ever done.

That's when I had my **THIRD** galaxy brain moment.

> That's your LOT for the year!

'Thanks, sir,' I said, my voice shaking, 'but I can't accept this honour.'

There was a loud, dramatic gasp. The Head's temper scale changed from a **TICKLED PINK** to an **AGHAST RASPBERRY**.

'This whole time I've been living a lie,' I said, my heart thumping so hard it was practically fighting to jump out of my mouth. 'You see, every school has a ranking system,' I explained, 'a list of the **BEST** and the **WORST**, of who's hot and who's not and, as a nerdy refugee kid, I was right at the bottom.'

I could feel every eye on me now. My voice trembling, I kept going.

'I was constantly being made fun of for coming from the **'WRONG'** place, eating the **'WRONG'** food, and wearing the **'WRONG'** clothes. I was sick of it, so I pretended to be someone who I wasn't so you would all like me and vote for me and I'm very sorry. So, as of right now, I resign from my position as school captain.'

Another wave of gasps rippled through the audience.

'There is someone who is way more worthy of this role than I am,' I continued.

Somewhere backstage, Humphrey smiled.

'JoJo, can you please come up here?' I asked.

Humphrey's eyes almost **POPPED** out of their sockets as a confused JoJo walked up on stage.

I took my sash off and put it over JoJo's shoulder, then turned to the audience.

'I think we can all learn something from this,' I said. 'Cool, nerd, weirdo, or even refugee. Aren't they all just **STUPID**, made-up boxes that we cage each other in?'

There was a murmur in the audience.

Did they agree, or were they all a bit tetchy because it was almost lunch time?

Anyhoo, they needed firing up. Suddenly I was a general, calling out to the rest of my troop to charge with me,

THEN LET'S BREAK FREE!

I yelled.

LET'S LIVE IN A WORLD WITH ZERO CLIQUES! WHERE BEING COOL IS BEING YOURSELF! STAND UP AND JOIN ME!

TOTAL SILENCE.

Everyone in the audience looked at each other like they were waiting for someone else to stand up first.

And then, that someone did.

One brave boy stood up from the crowd. A beacon of **HOPE** in a dismal crowd. Sometimes one person is all you need.

It reminded me of something the imam once said at Quran class: 'Whoever saves one person, it's as if he has saved all of Mankind.'

That's me. Kamal Noor. Saviour of Mankind.

Or so I thought.

The boy opened his mouth and screamed, **'PUKE BOY!'** and then everybody got up and started shouting it until all the teachers got to their feet and tried to quell it.

Totally **FREAKED** out, I decided to make a swift retreat and I hurried off backstage, not

forgetting to snatch *THE CHEAT BOOK* back from
a stunned Humphrey, gawping in the wings. I
blew a wet raspberry at him as I **ZOOMED** past
and burst through the back doors out into the
cool air of the playground.

What just happened?
I had everything I ever
dreamed of, the **WHOLE
WORLD** at my feet and
then the rug was pulled out
from under me by … me?
I was back on the social
scrap heap. *Do not pass Go,
do not collect £200.* But I was
actually … **OK?!**
The doors behind me swung
open and two familiar faces appeared.
'**THAT** was insane,' said Wing,
taking a seat next to me. 'You
dynamited your own reputation!'

219

'Don't listen to him, you did amazingly,' said JoJo, sitting down on the other side of me.

'You would say that – he made you school captain,' said Wing.

'Yeah, JoJo, about that,' I said. 'Don't get your hopes up. The school captain is a **POWERLESS** figurehead.'

'Oh?' exclaimed JoJo. 'Well, you don't have to be school captain to do something **GOOD** for the school.'

'True. But will they listen?' I sighed. 'You saw what happened back there. I tried to sink the cliques and got mocked.'

'You can't change the world **OVERNIGHT**, Kamal,' said Wing, 'but you can change yourself and eventually you might influence others.'

'Wow,' I said, 'that's wildly deep coming from you.'

'I have my moments,' said Wing, brushing off his shoulder.

'Well, **PUKE BOY** or **REFU-FLEA**, I don't care what people call me any more. I'm exhausted,' I said. 'I'm just happy to hang out with my two friends who call me Kamal.'

'To your face!' Wing smiled, nudging me. 'But are you sure you'll be OK going back to slurping the curd of nerd after tasting the sweet nectar of popularity?'

'Firstly, curd of nerd—? **EW!**' I said. 'And, secondly, if we're going to speak in rhyme, then I'd say that all I got from chasing likes was nonstop yikes. It really is lonely at the top and I'd much rather slum it on the bottom with you guys.'

'Thanks. I think?' said Wing.

'But still, your school captain speech really got me thinking,' said JoJo. 'What if there were no ratings?' She took her laptop out of her school bag and immediately got to work. 'I was thinking, a **BIG** part of the problem is PopStock dictating to us who is cool or not. We'd all be much better off without it,' said JoJo, feverishly tapping away at her keyboard with a **DEVILISH** grin. 'So, I came up with the perfect solution.'

After a flourish of keystrokes, JoJo proclaimed: 'WE ARE NOW ALL **FREE**!'

It was all quiet at first, then there was an annoyed **'UGH!'** in the distance that was quickly echoed by a chorus of irritation that swept through the school in a big wave of grumbling.

'JoJo! What did you just do?' panicked Wing.

'Oh, nothing much. I located PopStock's server, overwhelmed it with bots and **CRASHED** the app!' JoJo giggled.

I was expecting riots, meltdowns, or some kind of **UPROAR**, but after a wave of whingeing, everyone just shrugged, deleted the app and went to lunch.

Just like that, PopStock's reign of terror had ended. Not with a bang but a **'WHATEVER'**.

Natural order was restored: the cool kids at the top and everyone else at the bottom.

Being a dork again was not so bad. It had perks.

1. You can hang out with whoever you want.

2. Not be 'too cool' to do things you like.

3. Dance like no one's watching because they aren't.

4. Not worrying about being the person that everyone wants to be - you can... ...JUST BE YOU

As long as I had friends, I could handle anything.

And for the things I couldn't?

Well, I had *THE CHEAT BOOK.*

ACKNOWLEDGEMENTS

This book that you hold in your hands could not have gotten there without the help and support of a team of very awesome and talented people.

The first is my superstar agent, Rachel Petty! Thank you for generally being awesome, believing in the book and your help in finding it a home.

That home being the marvellous Hachette!

Ginormous props to my genius editor Nazima Abdillahi, whose creativity and insightful notes helped steer *THE CHEAT BOOK* in the right direction. Major props to the next level design work of Jennifer Alliston, whose fun & vibrant designs so perfectly nailed the cheekiness and mad energy of the book.

Epic high-fives to Krissi Hill & Jasmin Kauldhar who worked their marketing and PR magic.

Colossal kudos to Nic Goode in sales, Joelyn Esdelle in production, Annabelle El-Karim in Rights and Almaz Brooks in Audio for your super savvy and creative work.

Team Cheat Book is the best and I loved working with all of you!

This book would not have gotten into the hands of all these excellent people without the support of others that I must thank.

Huge thanks to Leah Thaxton and the FAB Prize for choosing my submission for the Second Prize back in 2017, which was the final push that led me to give permission to myself to pursue writing professionally.

The Cheat Book was originally written in Dapo Adeola's writer's clinic during his residency with the BookTrust. Much love to Dapo Adelola and

Rachael Davis for their enthusiasm, support and advice which spurred me to carry on with the book.

I'm tremendously grateful to writers like Laura Dockrill, Patrice Lawrence, Vinay Patel, Kieron Gillen, Non Pratt, Lucy Prebble, Nikesh Shukla, Cressida Cowell, Anna James and Neil Gaiman for their time and kind words of encouragement. It meant so much.

And last but not least, thanks to my friends and family for everything.

HOW TO DRAW KAMAL

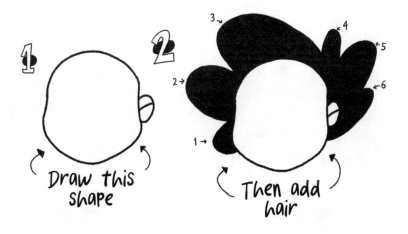

1 Draw this shape

2 Then add hair

3 Draw his face

Now go draw!